I0623911

We'd like to thank Jesh Art Studio for the incredible cover for this book, as well as our editing team, A Book a Day Author Services and Melanie Ulrich. Thank you for helping us bring Roxie to life!

DAGGER-FOR-HIRE

ROXIE ANDREWS

LORI COLLIER

1

Roxie

MOST PEOPLE GO through life sheltered, sure in the knowledge no one will betray them.

Not this girl.

My momma raised me to assume betrayal was always part of the landscape. She drilled it home to me and my brother to expect it like lightning during a thunderstorm.

Like the lightning that lit up the road now and hammered home the betrayal in the stark silhouette of deadly figures against the black night sky.

A normal person would say it was random. I was out in the middle of the woods with few structures around, except the handful of mountain cabins that dotted the side of the land-scape. A normal person would assume this was chance—a were pack out to hit up a passing motorist for their wallet. Or their car. Or worse.

I wasn't normal.

I was due at one of those cabins at any minute for a

midnight rendezvous to pick up a magical artifact for a risky courier job. They might know exactly who I was and where I was headed.

Could be they wanted to make sure I didn't get to my destination. Maybe there were more of them at the client's house relieving him of his relic at this very moment.

Not happening.

I let the car slither to a stop. The men blocking my car were wolf shifters if I guessed right. It was the way they stood, how their eyes leaked that hint of the animal behind the human façade.

That, and the hair. I don't know why they liked the look, but the wolf shifters I'd run into since we came to Colorado a year ago were always a little scruffy looking.

Personally, I liked my men clean shaven with just that little bit of stubble to let me know they could grow a beard if they wanted to. Stubble I can run my hands over.

These boys did nothing for me. They'd already closed in around the back of the car, encircling me like I was prey.

I was no one's prey. Whoever had sent these idiots hadn't sent enough.

We lived our lives as outcasts, but my mother was a warrior. She was the leader of the Illieri. Or at least, she had been before it all started.

Since we'd left before I came of age, I wouldn't ever come into my power as an Illieri but I was still my mother's daughter. Spending our life on the run had only made me stronger.

I looked at them through the glass. Their clothes were almost identical. Faded jeans and dark t-shirts that looked like maybe they'd worn them a few days in a row. Or weeks. They looked a little ripe.

But that wasn't all I saw. I saw their strengths and weaknesses. I catalogued any openings for taking them out. I saw the powerplay between them and knew what I might do to exploit it.

The biggest guy wasn't the alpha. The smallest dude claimed that title despite his size. Dominance among weres was funny that way. It didn't have to do with size. That guy might be small, but he was the one I had to watch out for.

Still, dominance didn't ooze off him in waves the way it did with some alphas and I wondered if he was in full control of his pack. It was a weakness I could turn to my advantage.

I didn't need to reach for weapons. I had knives strapped to my hips and thighs, and stakes in sheaths fitted to my upper arms.

Shifters didn't need staking the way a vamp did, but still, a stake to the neck or the heart would get the job done. I carried more stakes than knives lately, but only because we were short on cash from all the extra food my brother Dash had needed in the past few months.

I could make stakes myself for free.

The middleman who set up this job could have tipped them off that I was coming this way. I had worked for the dwarf before and trusted him as far as I trusted anyone in my world— which was to say, a troll's hair more than a stranger.

I didn't think my contact would have anything to gain from selling me out, but then, selling was the operative word there. He'd probably do just about anything for money. It was why he was so stingy with the cut he gave me, but when you weren't a legally registered dagger-for-hire, what could you do?

Too bad he didn't realize screwing me over meant a world of hurt for him. I'd take care of these assholes, finish the job so I could salvage my paycheck, then have a nice chat with my former business associate before going home to check on my little brother. All in a night's work.

I bunched my hair into the elastic I kept on my wrist and stepped from the car, keeping myself in the vee behind the door. Circling to try to keep them all in my sights wouldn't help in this situation. There were too many of them.

My bo staff would be handy but I never relied on the fickle hunk of supernatural wood. I couldn't call it to me on command, so it was nothing more than nice backup when it decided to show itself.

I scrunched my nose. They smelled like a griffon had pissed on a running shoe then left it to rot in the sun. I don't know if you've ever smelled griffon piss, or stale piss for that matter. The shit is rank.

Keeping my eyed on the alpha, I shook my head and gave them the courtesy of a warning.

"You'll want to move. Now."

The two skinny dudes flanked their leader while the two that resembled moving vehicles circled around the back of the car behind me.

I shrugged. "Okay, we do this your way."

I rubbed the knuckles of my left hand together as my right twitched, ready to move when they did. What had once been a nervous tick was now my way of prepping for battle. It steadied me for what was coming.

One of the men sniffed and ran the back of his hand under his nose, swiping at it. Another of them did the same, catching the gesture like it was a yawn.

It was gross, especially if you weren't a two-year-old kid, but it was also something else. It told me these were tweakers. They were sniffing Vampire Dust and that meant I might be a little sore after this. Fighting myths who were tweaking was a whole different level of fight.

The alpha launched himself at me, shifting in midair. He might be the smallest of them but he had a head a foot wide and jaws to match.

A were on Vamp Dust was faster and feral as hell. It was probably why I'd sensed the alpha wasn't fully in control.

It changed them physically, too. Right now, I was facing a wolf shifter that looked like a kid who got hold of his mom's scissors and gave himself a haircut. His hair was oily and dirty looking, and his eyes were red rimmed and crazed. His fangs were closer to a saber-toothed tiger's giant teeth than a wolf's.

Snot dripped from his nose, mixed with a tinge of red.

What kind of idiot first thought to himself, "let's take some of that ash you get when you stake a vamp and sniff that shit." You had to be sick to do that, right?

Moving fast, I shoved the door of the car wide at the last second and Alpha's face hit metal and glass with a satisfying crunch that would slow him down some.

The two behind the car hadn't shifted to their wolf forms yet. I crouched, throwing a knife at one of them. The sick squish and thunk of the knife as it met his flesh let me know I hit my mark.

Alpha wolf's foul breath heated the air seconds before he came around the door to my hidey hole, making me gag. Rotten meat and dog shit. Add in the rank smell wafting from his greasy coat and my stomach churned and spat bile at me, burning the base of my throat.

When Alpha jumped, big ass teeth aimed at my face, I turned and let his jaw sink into the stakes holstered at my upper arm. With a yank, I wrapped the car's seatbelt around his neck and pulled with everything I had.

Alpha gurgled as the seatbelt cut into his neck and I hissed the question I'd been dying to ask. "Who set this up?"

He pushed a broken "screw you" at me through my hold on his neck as I caught movement from the side. One of the skinny twins was barreling toward me, thankfully still in his human form.

I love when they were too dumb to know their momentum worked against them. I threw a back kick into his midsection, catching him as he plowed into me, the force of my foot stopping him dead in his tracks. He crumpled to the ground, arms tight around his middle, struggling for air much like his alpha.

A knife to the chest made sure he was out of this for good.

Alpha coughed and choked, but I couldn't hold up against his shifter strength. He was going to break lose soon. I dropped the seat belt and reached for another knife, jamming it into the side of his neck before I jumped over the body of the other one. That would hold the alpha for a bit until I could get back to question him.

"The island lady said to wait!"

I didn't know which one of the ones still standing shouted the words, but my blood did a deep freeze in my veins at those words.

Those words could only mean one thing. My world narrowed to a single fact.

Isle had caught up to us and it wasn't time.

We needed to go. Mom had seen a lot of conflicting things in her visions, but she'd always been clear on one thing. If the Illieri caught us, if we went back to them before Dash had reached his full potential, all would be lost. We had to stay ahead of them until he was strong enough. Until the time was right.

Wish she'd been a little clearer on exactly what that timing would look like, but Mom was like that. Dead sure on a lot, hella vague on even more.

I moved faster, pushing harder. What had been fun exercise a minute ago was now life threatening.

I aimed for the short scrawny guy, the weakest link, lunging and slashing with my blade as I passed, but he was fast and evaded my attack easily. Maybe not the weakest link after all. As he twisted to avoid the strike, he reached for me, but I wrenched away and threw my elbow out to connect with the side of his head.

He growled a warning as he started to shift. Spinning, I

swept for his legs with one of my own, but I only managed to make him stumble slightly before he righted himself. I nailed the side of his face when I came around the second time. A well-placed ax kick to the back of his head knocked him out completely.

Another one had shifted and was now on top of me, just as warped and cranked up on Dust as his alpha had been. He hurled me to the ground where gravel greeted me, removing a layer of skin on my back and shoulders.

His claws swiped at my abdomen, but I twisted, turning what could have been a devastating gutting into a torn shirt and some painful but not debilitating gashes.

I pulled my feet in close to my body and threw my hips straight up in the air, ignoring the searing pain in my midsection. I shoved and he went flying, but there was no time to do anything else. A hand clamped down on my wrist and wrenched me up as the cuts in my stomach screamed at me.

A hulking fist spun me and one of the big fuckers plowed a fist into my jaw. Pain sluiced though my head, reverberating in my skull.

I went down hard, face first, tasting the dirt next to the side of the road. My last knife went flying, far enough away that I didn't have a hope of getting it back until this was over.

I let out a shout and flipped over, but my head was still reeling and the big guy was on top of me before I could get the world back into focus.

I grabbed for a fist-sized rock a foot away from me and twisted when another of them came back into view. Long strands of drool falling from his maw told me he was looking forward to taking a chunk out of my ass as the other guy held me down.

They thought they could take me if they ganged up on me. Come and get it, asshole.

I thrashed and got a leg free, kicking out at the big guy's

face. His nose splattered open, spraying blood and he cupped his hands to try to stop the bleeding. Like that might help.

The wolf looked his way and I took the opening, swinging the rock at his head and not caring about the sickening crack. I felt the rock sink into something that wasn't meant to be battered this way, but I kept going. In battles like this, it's them or me.

It's never gonna be me. I slammed the rock into his battered skull— once, twice, again and again until he went down with a gnarly dent in the side of his skull that sported plenty of blood and a little brain matter in the mix.

With most of them on the ground, either unconscious or writhing in pain, I had one shot to get information out of them. I headed for the guy in human form whose nose I'd just broken.

Something else I was good at was making people talk when I had to. Apply a little pressure to that and he'd tell me who put them up to this.

I didn't make it. Tall and skinny had gotten up and was on me.

His arm snaked under my chin and I knew what he was doing, but it was too late. He locked me in a sleeper hold before I could stop him.

I tried to claw at his eyes, but he had his head tucked. I stomped at his feet, but he didn't seem to notice or care. Fucking shifter strength was a real bitch.

Spots formed at the edge of my vision. I raised an elbow and did my best to reach the side of his head, but there was no way to connect the way he had me pinned.

2

Roxie

I needed to end this. I grunted and smacked at his arm with my open hand, more a gut response than anything useful.

Giving up was not an option. It was *never* an option.

I clawed at his arm. I batted at his tucked head. I might as well be a fly.

With only seconds before I would lose consciousness, I felt a tingle in the palm of my right hand.

Thank fuck. I knew what that tingle meant.

I let out a sound that should have been a laugh but was garbled and choked as I pictured what was about to happen. I placed my fist up against his eye and waited as I watched the last little bit of light fade from my vision and hoped my bo staff would appear even if I wasn't conscious.

The staff shot out from my hand, its shaft piercing the wolf's eye and going straight through the back of his skull. He released me instantly and I staggered as I sucked in a breath, fighting to steady myself.

They were all out, that last guy laying on the ground with a hole through his head where his right eye had been. My stomach decided to spit at me again. I wished it would stop doing that.

The magic bo vanished, presumably because I was out of danger. It was like that, appearing only if I was in a fight for my life and vanishing when I was safe again. More than once, I wished it came with a note telling me who sent it and how the hell to control the damned thing.

No amount of meditation, focus, or creative swearing would bring it to me on command. Maybe my mom could have taught me to call it on command if she'd still been with us when it first showed up, but the mystery was beyond my abilities.

Would it have the guy's brain matter on one end the next time it appeared or would it be self-cleaning?

I was clutching my stomach and cursing as I rounded up what I could of my knives and stakes and started for the car.

Part of me wanted to go face off with the guy who'd set me up, just to take some small measure of revenge for what he'd just done to me but I didn't have that luxury. Right now, keeping Dash out of the Illieri's hands was more important than revenge. It was more important than anything.

***

I don't ever remember not having a go-bag packed. From day one, we had to be ready to leave at the first whisper that Isle or one of the other Illieri had caught up to us before the time was right.

Patching up my wounds with the few remaining magicked bandages we had and putting clean clothes on had taken long enough. Combat boots, jeans and a tank. Over this, I layered leather pockets and sheaths strapped to my legs and arms, and a magic relic strapped to the inside of one boot. Ironically the relic was a hidden pouch that carried other relics. All the items Mom and I had been able to collect over the years that might help us face what was coming.

I skipped my deep wine lipstick, a small concession to the fact I was running out of time.

As I crossed to the car, I called out for the dog, albeit quietly. I didn't want to shout my location to anyone who came along. "Ghost!"

I tried kissy noises.

No, I'm not a kissy noise person, but this puppy was damned cute.

I heard nothing in response.

Not that I could take him with us if he did come out of the brush. He wasn't my dog. For all I knew, he belonged to someone here.

But I could say goodbye.

Since he came by at least a few times a week for food, I filled several large bowls on the back steps with the discount puppy food I'd picked up on our last grocery run and scanned the yard again.

No sign of him.

Yes, it was stupid that I was worried about saying goodbye to a puppy when I had a hell of a lot more to worry about.

No, I didn't have a good explanation for my attachment to him and the hope for that one last cuddle before we left.

Truth was, I couldn't put this off any longer. I had hoped to do one or two more jobs here before moving on, but not only was Isle probably on our trail, it was time to get Dash to a pack that could help him with his shift.

I'd gotten Dash loaded into the car and as comfortable as he could be. My brother was in pain almost twenty-four seven nowadays, but his pain seemed semi-tolerable at the moment. He was getting ready to shift for the first time and it wasn't going well.

Mom had said I'd find who we needed in Austin, but that was all she'd been able to see. Still, it was something, and I'd figure the rest out.

I turned and looked at the car. My stomach ached where the wolf had cut it open, but it was more than that. We were headed for our last stop.

"Mom said we'd make our last stand in Austin," I said to no one in particular.

"Coming to a head," I heard clear as day in my mind. It was my mom's voice. She was gone, but her memory held strength still. I saw her standing tall and regal in my head.

When I was young, I half hoped our mom had just made everything up. That she was simply eccentric or even crazy. That this was some paranoid delusion in her head.

Any remnants of that fantasy blew up ten years ago when Isle caught up with us. When everything had gone to hell and we lost Mom, leaving me to raise and protect my brother.

At least I knew she wasn't crazy. Strong as hell, focused on what had to be done to save the world someday, and willing to sacrifice to make sure that happened but not crazy.

"You're ready for it, girl," her voice said again.

Her memory was a little more cheerleader and less drill sergeant than she'd been in real life. I grinned at the thought as I scanned the tree line for the dog I didn't own and grabbed the last of our packs to load into the car.

I needed to get Dash to the Austin safe house so he didn't have to deal with being in the back of a car while his body tried to withstand the pain of his first shift into a dragon.

Dash was egg-born and there weren't really records about those kind of dragons. At least none that I'd ever seen and it wasn't like I could ask anyone. Dash would be seen as a commodity to be bought and sold to the highest bidder.

One that our mother had stolen and that I'd hidden all these years.

No way in hell was I going to risk anyone finding out about him by walking into the local myth archives and asking for any information they had on egg-borns.

He groaned when I got in and started the engine. I wanted to get some fluids into him. Maybe once we got far enough out of town, I could stop for a cherry slushie. He usually drank those by the gallon. If that didn't tempt him, nothing would.

I eyed the broken side mirror where Alpha's head had hit. Driving cross country with that was an invitation for a cop to pull us over. How would that go? A woman with brown skin and a fake driver's license trying to explain a semi-conscious white boy in the back seat?

Yep. Should be fun.

I got back out of the car. Duct tape from the backpack made for a quick fix to hold that bad boy in place. Didn't look good but it should keep us from getting pulled over. As far as I was concerned, duct tape was as good as any magic.

"Go!" My imaginary Mom sounded a lot more like the woman who raised me this time.

I looked one more time for Ghost, watching for the sleek gray face of the chunky-headed pit bull.

Nothing.

"Damnit, dog." I shouldn't care. I turned away but didn't stop hoping for the rustle of leaves that would tell me he'd come.

Dash's breaths were heavy and labored when I got back in the car, but he seemed to be sleeping for now. He was stretched out in the back seat as best he could in the small space, with blankets tucked around him. His brow had a sheen of sweat on it and he turned, trying to stretch in his sleep, as though the pain might ease if he could just extend his legs at the right angle.

There was no more time. I slammed the car into drive and drove away, not looking in the rear-view mirror. I couldn't afford it. Mom's visions were in charge right now and they told me it was time to leave. Time to get to Austin where everything would change forever.

3

ROXIE

THE TURNOFF to the Austin safe house was hard to spot and I was glad we'd made it during the day. It would have been impossible to find at night.

The car groaned as the dirt drive sloped down, through the woods that had seen a few magic burns. There were parts of it that were just fine, but swaths ran through it where the trees were nothing more than dead husks.

Ruts pitted the road every few yards and at one point about halfway down, there was a drop of several inches.

I knew from past experience wards would have the house locked up tight. Wards that would only open with my blood or with Dash's. I didn't know who helped Mom set the wards, but they were powerful. Enough to keep wildlife, humans, and myths at bay for years. It was a feat for a very powerful witch or more likely an entire coven.

Mom would have left a stash of money in the house. Since we were down to nothing, we needed to find it fast. Then I'd have to find work. You didn't exactly hang out a shingle that said Dagger-for-Hire – All Jobs Considered, especially if, like me, you hadn't registered with the national dagger registry.

When people had problems with a myth, when they needed muscle and someone who knew all the players in the magical world, a dagger was a solution people could turn to. Daggers didn't get that name because we necessarily used them in our work, although we all used some kind of weapon. The term dagger came from the first mercenary hired to do work dealing with myths—Jack Dagger. He wasn't around anymore, but the name lived on.

Sometimes, we were hired to execute a find-and-destroy order put out for a dangerous myth. There were times I'd been hired to guard someone or something. I did a lot of courier jobs, shuttling a magic object from one person to another.

I was damned good at what I did so I knew I could eventually get work as a dagger wherever we went. Problem was, it always took time to get the word out in a new city if you weren't registered. And registering cost money. A lot of it.

Instead, I would need to hit the streets to make the kind of connections that might get me work.

The long dirt drive opened to a gravel parking area large enough for a few cars in front of a small cabin with a wide front porch. The windows were dark, same as the woods around the house. Silent, dark, and still.

"We're here, Dash," I said, turning to shake him awake.

His response was an unintelligible mumble.

My baby brother was tall and his fifteen-year-old body had recently started putting on more height and muscle in prep for his turn. It had been funny to see him tripping over the new inches when it started happening, but I wasn't laughing now that it looked like I'd have to carry his gangly ass when he was so much dead weight.

Putting it off, I stepped from the car and looked around. I

would get the house open and get some of our things inside before trying to wake him again.

Luckily, I hadn't started any of that yet. I might have missed the sound if I was shuffling bags or opening and closing doors.

It was slight. Just the near-silent whoosh of wings, but I recognized it. I looked up as the shadow dwarfed us.

I pressed my tongue against my top teeth, one hand going to a knife at my hip as I reached into the car and shook Dash again. He didn't do more than stir.

"Dash," I put a lot more shake into the shaking this time. I could feel the heat pouring from his body even through the heavy material of his sweats.

Now way he was waking up. I shut the door and locked it, with Dash still inside. Not that a locked car door would do much to keep out a dragon if they wanted in, what with the sharp rippy-rippy talons at the end of their feet.

I stood my ground as the dragon set down, a lot more softly than should be possible, but dragons were like that. The impossible was nothing unusual for them.

His scales were a range of blues from deep midnight to an almost silver color, with everything else in between dappled in there. He was monstrous and gorgeous all at once. Something about the shimmering scales made me want to reach out and stroke them. Hell if that was going to happen. Not unless it suited my purposes and helped me control the situation.

The gold of his eyes pulled my focus. I'd never seen eyes that color. Not on a dragon or any other creature, and he was using that to his advantage, keeping me trapped in his gaze. I purposefully shifted my focus away, not liking the feeling that he might be able to mesmerize me.

The wolf and witch with him were just as startling as his eyes. They leapt from his shoulders, landing on the ground beside him as though it was perfectly normal for a dragon to ferry other myths like he was a commercial airliner.

Most dragons I'd known were too damned arrogant to let someone ride them like a horse.

Magic whispered around the dragon, waves of blue light that sifted into a pale green as they surrounded his body, and then he was a man standing there. Tall and built like he was made to take on the world. His eyes stayed the same burnished gold, set in a tanned face with a strong, square jaw framed by military cut brown hair.

I had the strangest thought that it was a damned shame myths kept their clothes when they shifted instead of being naked like human stories mostly depicted.

And where the hell had that thought come from?

Magic floated around the witch in wisps of violet and silver, as she shifted from her magic form to her human form. She came out of it a slightly less magical looking version of what she'd been, her eyes no longer silver, but a startling blue. Hair that had been a near glowing white in witch form was now honey blonde.

The wolf followed suit doing his own swirly magic thing with brown and black mist that matched his coat. In human form, he was only a little shorter than the dragon. His sleek straight hair was almost black with eyes to match. He had his arms crossed and a scowl on his face that looked like it might be permanent.

He wasn't really scowling at me, so much as the world in general, and I was in the way. Too bad for him.

I kept my back to the car, vigilant for any more sounds behind me or above me.

Power rolled off the dragon, potent and intense. Power that had me wary. I was here to find a pack for Dash, but I had to choose that pack carefully. And showing up with a witch and a wolf on his back seemed wrong.

"This house has been empty for years," he said, not offering his name.

A hint of accusation sullied his tone, almost as though he thought we should have shown up to claim the place sooner.

Or that he thought we shouldn't be there.

Whatever.

The fingers on my right hand flexed by my leg. If I needed to, I could have one of my knives out and thrown before they could reach us, and I wondered if he'd purposely set down far enough away that I'd feel like I had a shot.

Was that to lull me into a false sense of security or did he not want me to feel threatened?

I could have told him the house belonged to our mother, but I didn't offer the information. It's not like I could prove it if I needed to. When Isle caught up to us ten years ago, Mom pushed Dash and I out to make a run for it as she tried to fight Isle off. The deeds had been left behind, same as all the fake IDs she'd set up for us.

We worked our way through the houses Mom set up one by one over the last ten years, never staying in one spot for very long. There hadn't been a welcoming committee to challenge us at any of the others.

The dragon seemed unfazed by my silence. "I'm Adak and this is Tag and Aster. Our pack lands are near here. We saw movement and wanted to make sure no one was around who shouldn't be."

I didn't offer our names, first or last. Our last name had been Andrews since that battle with Isle, too, complete with fake IDs to back that up, but these people didn't need that information.

I would bet their lands were in a stretch of acreage on the northwest side of Capital of Texas Highway, the road we'd just taken on our way into town. It wasn't at all far from here.

I'd felt the ripple of magic as we passed that told me there was a magic fold there among the woods and rockface. My guess was that they lived in the fold, hidden away from humans and even some less aware myths.

Right near our land. The ward our mom had put on the house obviously didn't stretch to the property since they'd entered it without my permission. They might not be able to enter the building, but they could come onto our land. That wasn't going to work for me.

I added wards to the property to the list of things I'd need to buy with my first paycheck.

I let my hips loosen just a little, letting the natural sway of my body draw his attention, hopefully pulling the dragon or maybe one of the others off their guard. A small shrug of my shoulders drew attention to my shoulders and chest, the neckline of my tank. "Stay off our land and we gonna get along just fine."

I slid my tongue over my top teeth again, keeping my eyes locked to the dragon.

I saw his eyes scan my body and I knew I had him, but from one second to the next, his demeanor changed. He'd sensed Dash. I saw him scent the air and knew he would confirm Dash's presence. No way he'd miss the scent of another dragon.

Well, hell.

Those gold eyes narrowed with laser focus on me, accusation in the look. "He's in pain. You need to get him to his pack to help him with the change."

I gave a single shake of my head and took a step closer to the car door as I palmed a dagger at my back. The wolf growled, still in his human form, but no less threatening than if he'd had his furry face on.

Oh hell no. I might not have been here two minutes, but this was our land. No one was going to threaten me here or anywhere else.

I growled back, showing them strength instead of seduction as I showed my teeth. "You let me worry about him."

The look the dragon gave me was inscrutable but the tick in his jaw gave away his anger. "You're not doing him any favors. Dragons are meant to pack up. A pack can take on part of the pain for him. They can help speed up his first shift so he doesn't suffer."

No kidding. And I'd get Dash a pack, but I wasn't foolish enough to randomly choose a dragon pack and turn Dash over to them.

"We'll manage." I lengthened my spine not willing to let them get near Dash.

I thought I heard the dragon curse under his breath and he continued to stare in the direction of the back seat where Dash lay, even though I doubted he could see much of him through the car windows.

He took a step our way, but I stepped toward him, making it clear this was going to get violent if he persisted. He stopped himself, his eyes meeting mine. There was pain there, like it hurt him to know Dash was in pain.

"You have no idea what you're asking him to endure," the witch put in. Incredulity and accusation heavy in her voice.

The same accusation and shock I saw in all of them.

The witch continued, stepping forward. "It's selfish for you to keep him away from his pack, no matter your relationship. A girlfriend can't replace a pack."

I didn't correct her on our relationship.

The girl was wrong about more than just our relationship, though. She thought I couldn't understand what he was going through, but I knew the pain he was in. I'd watched the shaking, the way his muscles clenched, the groans that slipped out when Dash could no longer hold them back. I'd give anything to stop that pain, to see the easy going smile he usually wore back in place.

That wasn't an option just yet. Not until I was sure I found the right pack. Everything was riding on this.

I didn't know if the myths in front of us could feel Dash was different or not, and I didn't really want to find out. An egg-born dragon was a rare thing—a dragon not born from myth parents but created by the magic of three powerful covens wound together. It required a hefty sacrifice to balance the creation of a new myth. A life for a life.

If Mom's premonition was right, my baby brother was the most important dragon the world would ever know. More importantly, he was my family. I couldn't just ask the first pack we came across to take him in. I had to make this decision carefully for Dash.

I didn't know why a dragon, witch, and wolf would be traveling together. The dragon had said, "our lands." I'd never heard of a pack that had more than one species, much less three, in it.

That sounded more like a gang to me and that had to be bad news.

The dragon called Adak watched the car, gold eyes locked in as I moved my hand to the hilt of the knife on my right hip, blading my body—one foot in front of the other, my body turned at an angle to them in preparation.

Seconds passed. I didn't move. Didn't blink.

With a grunt, the dragon turned away again. He looked back at me over his shoulder. "Give him valerian root tea for the cramping. It will help."

And then magic swallowed him again, transforming him into the shimmering blue beast. The wolf and witch argued with him. I heard it in their tone even though I couldn't make out the words from their position on the other side of beast who now stood between us. He gave a low growl and even I could feel the command in it. There was power there and I knew it would wash over them the way it washed over me.

They weren't idiots. They listened to the dragon's order, shifting in midair as they leapt to his back.

I didn't know how they thought they'd take flight from here. Dragons needed a high perch to leap from to catch flight.

Color me shocked as I watched the dragon make a motion that looked like he was climbing a flight of steps into the air. First one foot, then the other. And damn if he didn't do just that, climbing invisible steps right in front of me.

When he'd made it five or so dragon-sized steps up into thin air, he gave a shove with one enormous back foot that launched him into the air. I watched as they dropped for a split second before the wind caught his wings and they shot up. He winged north toward the fold that was too damned close for comfort to our new cabin.

I watched and wondered how many other dragon packs there were in Austin, because surely whatever crazy gang this was, they weren't the ones for Dash.

4

Adak

ASTER AND TAG were silent as we flew back to the lair, which was a good thing. I needed the quiet to process what we'd just seen.

There were occasionally dragons adopted into human families—usually kids no one realized were dragons until they began their first shift—but those families were usually eager to find help for their kids and turned to the nearest pack.

I hadn't gotten a look at the dragon in the car back there, but if he was headed into his first shift, he had to be in his teens.

The woman had been older. Not old enough to be his mother. Maybe a sister? Or friend?

I felt a growl I didn't intend roll through my chest at the thought she might be his girlfriend. The thought was ludicrous with how young the dragon was compared to her, but that wasn't why the growl had come. It was the idea of the woman with someone.

I growled again, this time at myself. I didn't know what the hell was happening, but I didn't like it.

We entered the fold that protected Nova Force from the outside world and I set us down in the field outside the lair, shifting as soon as we did.

Of course, Aster didn't just drop the issue and let me walk away in peace.

"Are we just going to leave him with her?" She asked, jogging to keep up with me as I strode to the front porch.

"What would you have me do? Kidnap the boy?"

Tag grumbled something about that not being a bad idea. I ignored him.

The fierce way the woman had protected the dragon was impressive, if stupid. She was human but she'd stood her ground, ready to take on a dragon, witch, and wolf shifter to protect him.

"We should try to speak with him," Aster persisted. "She has no right to make that decision for him."

I stopped when we reached my office door and turned, biting back yet another growl. The young witch meant well.

"I'll try to talk to her again."

I didn't give them a chance to continue, shutting myself in my office.

That property had stood empty for years. It grated on my nerves having it near our pack lands without any idea why the house was so heavily warded. I'd taken to flying over it whenever I came in and out of the pack fold from that direction, always watching to see if someone showed up.

And she had. She didn't look or act like most humans I knew. I'd bet she was a dagger. Even in the realm of daggers, she would stand out. Most humans working as daggers carried guns. A lot of them.

She had the quantity thing down, but she went with blades and stakes instead of guns. A bold move that required hand to hand combat instead of firing weapons from a distance. The way she held her body told me she knew how to use them, too. They weren't for show or intimidation.

A witch couple sold the property seventeen years ago, almost to the day. They moved out of the state, only telling friends and neighbors they received a great offer on the property and were retiring. I remember my grandfather was bothered when no one moved into the house and the wards popped up overnight to keep anyone from entering it.

The woman I'd just met must be in her mid-twenties at most, so she hadn't bought the house or placed the wards. I was tempted to shift and flyover the property to see if she'd managed to get through them. Maybe she didn't know about the magic protecting the cabin. Hell, maybe the house wasn't even hers and she was about to get a nasty shock trying to break into it.

I started my computer and pulled up email, choosing to ignore the arrival of the fledgling dragon and his guardian and checking for reports from returning teams instead. If a patrol team had something urgent to report, they came straight to my office. If they had anything that wasn't urgent but might be of interest to me, they emailed, copying the other alphas of Nova Force.

When a knock sounded on my door seconds later, I knew it was Lesande. I could smell the leader of Nova Force's witch coven through the door. Tag, the third leader of Nova Force, was with her.

So much for him knowing when to leave well enough alone.

"Tell me about our new neighbors." The tall blond witch I'd first met when she and Tag and I served in the military together entered the room and took a seat across from me.

She never went for coy or casual. Lesande was straight forward and blunt as hell. It was one reason she was so skilled at leading Nova Force's coven of sixty-one witches. It was also why she and I managed to work together so well.

Leading a pack made up of three species had never been done before and it wasn't easy. But we had our reasons for doing it and we made it work. If Tag, Lesande, and I hadn't been strong heads to begin with, we couldn't do it. As it was, when we announced our plans to merge our packs into a single force with me as the ultimate alpha over all three species, we'd each lost members.

A few of my dragons went to Heritage Pack, the dragon pack with territory to the south of us. Good riddance. Anyone willing to join Heritage Pack were bigoted assholes I didn't need in my pack. Others went out on their own to find new packs or go rogue.

Some of the witches left and formed a smaller coven, living up in Leander now, outside our territory.

There were wolf shifters that left and lived as loners or joined packs up in Oklahoma.

Most had stayed, though, and those who'd stayed with us were loyal to a fault. They were good people.

I didn't open my eyes as I answered Lesande. "Tag already told you all I know, I'm sure."

She snorted indelicately, never one to hold back her feelings. "I have his impressions. Now I want yours."

I opened my eyes and sat up. It was a fair request. She might not have the final say on pack decisions, but she was as concerned with the safety and well-being of the pack as I was.

I didn't answer her, though. Instead, I looked at Tag. "What were your impressions?"

He met my gaze, eyes thoughtful. Tag was the youngest of us all, but that didn't make him any weaker. The wolf shifter was a hell of a force to be reckoned with. He'd come back from our service in the war to find his alcoholic uncle had run their pack damned near into the ground.

It hadn't been easy, physically or mentally, given the history between him and his uncle but Tag had challenged him and taken the pack.

"The dragon was early in his first shift," Tag said. "I couldn't scent much more than that." He frowned. "Though he was young, I think."

I agreed. "He seemed young to me, too." Dragons could enter their first shift anywhere from sixteen to twenty years of age, but I would bet he was at the lower end of that range. "I couldn't tell much more than that off him, either."

My thoughts went back to the woman. "Those knives weren't for show."

It had been in the way she moved, how she positioned herself. The way her arms hung at her sides, not tense, but ready for a battle.

But it was more than that. "Blood." I looked at Tag. "You smelled it? Her gear wasn't filthy or anything, but I could smell the remnants of previous fights in the leather of her sheaths."

Tag gave a single nod.

"Tag said she was human?" Lesande pushed. "Powerful human?"

I nodded at that. She was human, for sure, but there was more to her than we were seeing.

Lesande divided a look between the two of us. "Do we need to worry about them being so close to the pack lands? Now that someone's shown up to claim the place, we can offer to buy it."

She was right. Buy the land and house and be done with them. It was the right thing to do for the pack. To get these unknowns away from our lands, our young.

I stood. "I'll see her in the morning. She'll take a cash offer."

5

It took forever to find the stash in the house, but the ward on it opened with my blood, same as the front door had.

The crack of the floorboards in the back hall when they let go their hold on the studs was shotgun loud in the quiet cabin. I angled the flashlight into the hole and pulled out a stack of what I hoped would be money wrapped in tight plastic. With the kind of jobs Mom did back when she set this all up, she'd been able to leave a little money for us at most of the safe houses.

A wider packet held papers and a book. I took the time to put the floorboard back into place and then carried the stacks to the worn wood kitchen table.

I liked this house a lot more than some of the others we'd lived in, despite the weight of Dash's first turn and knowing I'd have to choose a pack for him here.

The kitchen table was a large wood farm table that made

me think of family. Of more than what we'd ever had as far as family went.

Someone left a paint mark in the shape of a fingerprint on one edge of the table and it was easy to imagine it as Dash's when he was little if we'd grown up like normal people. Or maybe a cousin— one we'd run through the woods with or played in the yard with until we were called in to dinner.

I think Dash's shift was addling my brain and making me wish for things that wouldn't ever be true.

I pulled a knife from my hip and slit the coverings on the packages, feeling the tightness in my chest ease a little when the first one proved to be money. I fingered the stacks and guessed it was a few thousand there. Whenever Mom set up safe houses, she bought them outright so this would go mostly toward utilities and food. It would last a little while.

I always filled our table with the kinds of foods that held up well to the magic surges that took out some of the more delicate crops. We didn't eat a lot of fruits as those were hard hit by magical burns, but tubers and hardier grains did well and wouldn't break the bank. And canned meats. Beans. It wasn't fancy, but it got the job done.

Before the Dawning, myths had to keep their numbers low to be able to hide the truth of their existence. And then they were too busy fighting during the Dawn Wars that followed to have babies. But when the war ended, myths were able to come out of hiding. If you didn't have to hide, you could build bigger families. Build a life. And they did. The world's population of myths is thought to have increased five-fold or more over two decades.

The increase in magical beings on the planet caused waves of magic to flow in unpredictable intervals, burning and killing plant life.

It affected the cost of crops and scientists warned if we

didn't stop the waves, it would eventually lead to such a decrease in plant life that it would affect the air quality and more. The warnings ranged from portentous to downright ominous.

I needed to check out the woods around us and see if there were animals I could hunt, but I wasn't sure there would be anything. While our cabin had enough of a wooded plot around it that it felt isolated, there were some big housing developments along this stretch of road. They probably chased away most of the wildlife when they built those.

The other stack of papers included the deed to the property and house, thank the Goddesses. I didn't know why she'd hidden this deed here instead of having it with her like she had all the others, but maybe she'd seen that she wouldn't be with us by now. Either way, I'd feel a lot better chasing people off our land if I knew I could prove it was ours.

I fingered the book, running my hands over the soft leather cover and the dragon etched into its smooth surface. I opened it, my heart jumping a bit at the idea that it might be a journal written by our mom filled with things she wanted us to know. It was empty. Flipping through the hand cut pages showed nothing but blank page after blank page.

I set it aside and lifted the last of the items in the stack. An envelope. The tingle I felt when I touched it told me there were wards in place to protect it.

I used my knife to pierce the skin on the inside of my forearm and let a few drops of my blood spill onto the seal. When that opened the envelope, I looked back to the journal and, pulling it close again, dropped a little blood onto a few of the pages.

Nothing. She really had left me a blank journal.

I slid a single page out of the envelope and opened it, recognizing the writing at once. The letter wasn't soft and mushy or sentimental, but I could hear Mom's voice in my head as I read it.

Roxie,

If you're reading this, you've done it. You made it as far as Dash's change. I always knew you could. He needs a pack now, and that's something you'll have to help him with. I never saw anything about his pack. Trust your instincts. You'll know what's right for him.

For now, you need to find work. See a shifter named Hunt Gentry. You'll find him north of the city. He'll help you find work.

I unfolded a torn piece of a map with a small x in one spot. I hoped that was Hunt's location and not some note about a weapons shop mom hoped to visit someday.

My visions never filled in much about what would come once you made it to Austin, but I can tell you this: you need the goat and the young ones. You and Dash won't make it through the end of this without them.

Stay strong, my warrior.

Mom

Fate didn't give me time to sit with any of that. The sound of retching hit my ears and I was moving down the hall before I really processed what was happening.

The smell hit me as soon as I entered the bedroom and found Dash hanging over the side of the bed. If he'd been throwing up before this, or even showing signs he might throw up, I'd have put a garbage can there. I hadn't, so the puke was now splashing onto the floorboards and up onto the sides of the bed and nightstand. No point in putting a bucket there now.

I went to the foot of the bed and crawled up it to get behind Dash.

"Way to christen the place, bro."

His forehead didn't feel any hotter than it had been when I pushed the hair out of his face, but that wasn't saying much considering how hot it had been for the last few days. It hadn't gotten any cooler.

I had no idea if vomiting was normal or if this meant things were getting worse. Maybe this was all wrong. Maybe this wasn't at all the way this first shift was supposed to go.

The heaving slowed and Dash sank back onto the bed. I took a dirty t-shirt and wiped his mouth and chin before tossing it across the room. We didn't have a washer and dryer in the cabin but I could wash it in the sink and hang it out on the porch railing.

"I'll clean that up," Dash croaked, making me laugh. It was probably what he'd intended. Goddess, I wished I could make this better for him.

"Let's hope we have cleaning supplies here somewhere."

"Money?" Dash asked, his eyes still closed.

"Floorboards. And the name of some guy Mom said I could go to for work."

Dash started under my hand at that news and I understood the reaction. She'd never left us the name of any friends before.

"She said we'd need the goat and the young ones." Mom's visions had never been crystal clear. Often it was a feeling and not much more. Like, the way she was absolutely sure about Dash saving the world someday. It wasn't that she saw him saving the world. It was a feeling.

Dash snorted. "A goat would be nice."

"For milk or for meat?" I asked. If we slaughtered the goat it would only take Dash a day to go through the meat at the rate he was going nowadays.

Apparently, the hope of milk or meat wasn't enough to keep him awake. I heard his breathing level out and slipped from the bed to find something to clean the mess with. I should have a clean garbage can or bucket waiting for the next time. Scrubbing puke off the floors wasn't my idea of fun.

And much as I didn't want to do it, I needed to go see this Hunt guy. A few thousand dollars was nice to have, but with the cost of food, that wouldn't last us long. If Hunt wouldn't or couldn't help us, it could take me weeks to make the kind of connections I needed to get jobs coming in.

I looked back at Dash. I had to leave him one way or the other. We needed food and supplies. I'd eaten the last can of beans for breakfast, but we needed to restock the pantry and, goat or no, he needed meat.

If the cabin didn't reek of vomit despite my efforts to clean and air the place out, it might have been harder to leave an hour later. I drove north toward the area on the map clipping. It was a place north of Austin called Leander, a location I'd heard a lot of myths lived in.

Most places in the world, the International Alliance Council with its panel of humans and myths was in charge, and humans and myths lived together in what was becoming increasingly tenuous peace.

For the most part, countries were willing to bend to the governance of the council, but the magic waves had started the fighting up between humans and myths again, so much so that a lot of people had dubbed this the Second Dawn Wars. People questioned whether the Council would be able to maintain control. If they couldn't, I didn't know who could. The myths on the Council were the most powerful in the world, both politically and magically.

But there were pockets of areas that were predominantly human controlled, and others controlled and populated by myths. Leander was a myth haven.

Twenty minutes later, I was pulling onto a dirt road I thought would take me to the little x on the map. I was reasonably sure, anyway. The problem was, maps weren't always updated when an upheaval happened after a magic burn.

Sometimes the magic burns only scorched crops and plant life on the surface. Other times, the damage went yards deep into the soil and caused craters or tossed chunks of earth and buildings far and wide, destroying anything that happened to be in the way.

There were whole areas up this way that looked to have gone through the upheaval type of burn in years past and the woods now grew up around and through the wreckage. I eyed a tree that held the remnants of a chain link fence tangled fifteen feet up in its boughs, the branches hugging the metal as though it were part of the tree itself.

I checked the map again and kept going. I was reasonably sure I had the right general direction, but I might have to abandon my car up ahead and hoof it through the crazy half woods, half trash pile to get far enough west to locate this Hunt guy.

"This better be worth it, Mom."

I wasn't at all ready for the wolf that jumped in front of the car like he had a death wish and was prepared to make his dreams come true on the grill of my 2001 sedan.

For the second time that week I faced a roadblock that likely wasn't friendly and cursed. Wolves were becoming a nuisance in my world.

When the wolf hopped up, putting his front paws onto the hood of my car, I found myself growling at him through the windshield. Because fuck that.

Before I could open the door, he was down and shifting faster than I'd seen a wolf shift in probably ever.

Once black hair now tinged with gray hung into his face but he flicked it back and I saw light green eyes, a full gray beard, and tanned skin. Despite the gray, I'd have put the guy someplace in his fifties if he was human.

Knowing he was a shifter meant he was in his late hundreds. The guy had seen some shit. Hell, he'd seen *the* shit.

He'd been alive long before the Dawning happened and had seen the fighting that followed.

Didn't mean I wouldn't take him down if he didn't get the hell out of my way. I shouted out to him. "Looking for Hunt Gentry."

He squinted at me and I held his gaze as he took me in. Still, when my name fell off his lips, I was more than a little stunned.

"S'cuse me?" I opened the door and stepped out.

"You're Roxie. Your mother said you'd come someday. I didn't think it'd be this soon."

I got the sense he meant the words to cut like it was somehow my fault, my failure, that brought us here so soon. He might be right but I wasn't going to dwell on that.

"You're Hunt?" I demanded. I didn't like playing games.

He gave a single nod. "Leave the car."

He didn't give me much time but I grabbed my backpack and locked the car before trekking after him. He'd all but disappeared into the woods and didn't seem overly concerned with whether I was keeping up.

If my stomach and shoulders weren't still sore from the wolf shifters, I'd love the chance to get a workout in as I vaulted logs and ran over the rough terrain. The magicked bandages I used before we left Colorado had done a lot to help, but I was still sore as hell.

When I caught up to him, we were in a small clearing in front of a tiny cabin with a little shed and a stack of wood next to it. The man stood in front of the cabin, watching me as I took in what I guessed was his home.

It was strange for a wolf shifter to live alone like this. Could he really be in his right mind if he lived alone? Wouldn't insanity take over soon enough? Unless insanity was the reason he wasn't in a pack.

His eyes seemed steady and sane, if I was any kind of judge on that. I wasn't sure I was.

"Mom told me you might have work when I got here."

His brows winged up. "Been talking to your mom lately, huh?"

His tone said he knew that was impossible, so I guess word had reached him somehow about the battle with Isle that took Mom from us.

I only raised my brows at him. He knew damned well I hadn't talked to her. Did I really need to explain every damned thing to this man?

He shifted his questioning. "Have you met your neighbors yet?"

Guess I shouldn't have been surprised he knew where the cabin was, too. Maybe he helped set up this safe house. Maybe he'd been there when the wards were set and tuned to our blood.

I remembered Mom pricking our fingers to take the blood when I was a kid and Dash was only a baby, but I didn't have any memories of the house or the magic that created the wards.

"Adak stopped by with a welcome basket." Okay, so he hadn't come bearing any gifts, but whatever.

"He's loyal to his force. A good man." Hunt said this with a nod like I'd asked what he thought of him.

I didn't get to answer. I heard the moan from the shed at the same time he must have. He moved as I shifted to a fighting stance, a blade in each hand.

But he hadn't come toward me as I thought he would. Instead, he went to the shed and opened the door.

I didn't know who—or what—I'd heard in the shed but wouldn't he want to hide it from me? Convince me he didn't have someone locked up in there or take me out before I could run off and tell his secret.

Not that I would. If he was holding someone in that shed, I wasn't the kind of woman to run and get help. I'd take care of him myself and get his prisoner out of there.

I moved quickly, settling myself behind him and to the left a little so I could see past him and into the dark space.

Only it wasn't a dark space. It might be a shed on the outside, but it was finished out on the inside. The paint on the inside was a light gray. Soft lights glowed from the ceiling and a bed took up most of the space.

It was what was on the bed that had blinking.

It was a little shocking to watch Hunt go into the shed and put a hand to the zombie's chest, laying it back down on the bed. The zombie looked like all the others I'd seen. Sort of like a walking corpse. His flesh wasn't exactly hanging off him all over, but you could tell it was dead on his bones and I knew from experience, it could indeed slough off in chunks if you rubbed too hard. His eyes had that cataract white glaze over them and chunks of hair and scalp had fallen out in patches.

Hunt opened a small cooler in the corner of the space and took out a hunk of meat the size of a football and handed it up to the creature.

Everything I knew about zombies said this was all wrong. They were faster than even a shifter and hell bent on destruction and violence. You sure as hell couldn't contain one in a small shed or appease it with a slab of deer meat or whatever the hell that had been.

Hunt re-secured the door then pointed at me. "You didn't see that. No one needs to know he's out here."

I raised my brows and kept the knives in hand, not willing to agree to anything where a zombie was concerned. What the ever-loving hell was a wolf shifter doing with a zombie?

He heaved a sigh and rubbed at his forehead, looking around the clearing. I could swear he mumbled something about letting people near them and what a mistake that was. Yeah, I was feeling the mistake, too.

"Nice pet." Yes, I should have kept my mouth shut. Sometimes my internal filter was an utter failure.

Hunt growled, deep in his chest. The kind of growl that would tell even the most clueless of humans he wasn't one of them. "He's not a pet."

"Noted." This was the guy who was supposed to help me find work? "Can't you find a vampire fury to take him off your hands?"

Zombies were what happened to a male vampire within days of turning. They were every bit as much of an abomination as vampires, only more so. They functioned for anywhere from hours to three days as a vampire but after that, their minds went to hell, literally turning into a gelatinous blob. They maintained the speed and power of a vampire but they were mindless killing machines that could only be controlled by a vampire.

They got the rep as brain eaters because they used their teeth more than anything else to take out anything they were pointed at, and that often involved chewing through the faces of their victims like they were trying to get to the chewy goodness of the inside of one of those runny chocolate egg things people make a big deal out of at Easter.

It was common for a fury of female vampires to keep zombies as weapons. They liked being able to wield their bloodthirsty power and vampires were powerful and fast enough to control zombies so long as the fury was large enough.

Come to think of it, how was it possible he controlled that thing and contained it in a flimsy outbuilding? There were usually silver chains and shit like that involved in keeping zombies.

Hunt wasn't impressed with my suggestion. His scowl told me as much before he did. "He's my brother. It took me years to get him away from the vampire bitch who made him. He's not going back until I'm dead and cold in the ground."

I looked again to the shed then raised my hands in surrender then realized I still had my knives in them.

"Sheathing these now," I muttered as I tucked them away. "How did they turn a shifter?"

It shouldn't be possible. The magic in a shifter's body—or in any myth's body—wouldn't allow them to become a vampire or zombie.

Then it dawned on me. "He was a—" I stopped myself before I said dud and went with the more politically correct term. "He was a quirk?"

Hunt gave a short jerky nod.

I gave a last look toward the shed then dismissed the zombie brother as none of my damned business. "About about that work?"

Hunt didn't look like he had any entrepreneurial spirit.

He was busy eyeing me up and down. "You're smaller than I thought you'd be."

"Yeah, I didn't get her size. I know." Mom was six three, but I'd stopped growing at six feet.

"You get any of her skill?" He picked up a stick and toyed with it.

"Some," I said. It was an understatement. I'd gotten a lot of my mom's skill. And what hadn't come naturally to me, she drilled into me over the course of nearly two decades of brutal training sessions.

Dash had been next to me for some of those sessions, but he was young. Only five when Mom fell to Isle. It was always a given that he would be the one to need protection. He would be vulnerable once his shift started and it was my job to protect him.

Hunt caught me off guard. He moved fast, not shifting, but employing the speed that came naturally to a wolf. I sidestepped, taking the hit but lessening the blow so that it glanced off my side.

Years of training had me reacting without thought. I blocked a haymaker he swung at me with a little too much ease. He couldn't be that bad a fighter. He wouldn't have survived as long as he had by telegraphing his moves so much.

He started this but I was sure as hell going to finish it. As I blocked his blow, I twisted down, spiraling to the side for an uppercut.

He never saw it coming if the spit that flew from his mouth as I nailed him in the jaw was any indication. And then for a few seconds, it looked like he was no longer holding back. Maybe I'd pissed him off with that last hit. Or maybe he'd just been warming up.

He unleashed a rein of punches to my head and body. I twisted one way and the other, trying to guard my vital organs.

Then I sacrificed, taking a nauseating hit to the kidney to gain some position so I could reach his head. I linked my hands behind it and pulled him down into my knee, driving it up into his face with all the force I had. The grunt that came out of him let me know I'd done some damage. He pushed back on my shoulders, catching his breath and I felt something shift in the air.

He was stopping the fight with the same suddenness he'd started it with.

He eyed me carefully as he stepped away before giving an almost imperceptible nod. Was that an acknowledgment of my skill?

"Not bad."

Excuse the hell out of me?

I ran the back of my hand across my lip, looking down at the blood. I didn't want to look at the damage to my stomach. I knew any healing from the magicked bandages was gone.

"That was a job interview?"

The asshole didn't notice that I was pissed. Or didn't care.

He shrugged his response.

I'd like to say I didn't roll my eyes.

I did. I rolled them hard. And he was lucky that was all I did.

He ignored the gesture and kept talking like this hadn't been a freaky visit to crazy town.

"Go see a hedge witch named Vivian. She's on the south side of Austin, off Brodie Lane. Look for the big purple house with the Christmas trees in the front yard."

I didn't ask why a hedge witch would have Christmas trees. Whatever floated her boat and all that.

"What am I seeing her for?"

"She's been poking around for someone to take on a job. Doesn't want to go through the usual channels."

I wondered what the usual channels were around here, but he kept going before I could decide if I should ask or not.

"Far as I know, no one's brave enough to take her up on it yet."

Probably because hedge witches could be irrational as fuck, if not a little crazy.

"But watch your ass, Roxie. Taking a job as an unregistered dagger in Austin is dangerous."

Tell me about it. Being unregistered was never a cake walk. It meant whoever hired you might not pay up at the end of the job. It meant you didn't have any credentials to flash if you had to enter private property to chase down a mark. And of course, there was always the chance someone else would poach your job before you could finish it.

But registering as a dagger cost more than a new car. Not a license I'd be buying anytime soon.

I waved off his warning. "Yeah, I got it."

He gave a shrug and turned without a goodbye, going into the house.

"Hey, do you know anything about goats?" I called behind him.

He didn't answer.

I eyed the shed again and wondered how the hell he kept that thing in there without a padlock or serious alarm system or something. At least Dash and I weren't too close to Leander. Maybe when that thing got loose, the zombie apocalypse wouldn't make it down our way.

6

I STOPPED at home to check on Dash. Given who showed up, I was glad I did.

The house still had its ward, but I'd rather I was around to protect him from anyone who might be able to get through it.

Three black trucks pulled in seconds after I arrived. The door to the first one opened and a large man who looked like he'd once been all muscle but had started to go soft around the belly like that doughboy character stepped out.

His glance at me was dismissive, at best. He moved toward the house as though he thought he could move right on past me.

Not happening.

I stepped in his path, hand going to a knife on my hip. My knives were getting a real workout lately. "We're not seeing visitors right now."

His gaze traveled the length of my body in that oh-so-creepy way a lot of men seemed to learn at some point in their lives. "We're here for the dragon."

I snorted and voiced the thought I'd had seconds before. "That's not happening."

I didn't have to guess how they knew Dash was here. This guy must be a dragon. The longer Dash was here, the more dragons would begin to sense his presence.

A man and woman stepped out of one of the other two vehicles and flanked the doughboy with the dark hair. These two had equally dark looks and matched his military style with black cargo pants and dark gray shirts.

Doughboy seemed to reassess me, eyes going wide that I'd have the audacity to dictate to him.

"He's a dragon. He belongs with his own kind," he growled.

I kept my face still in the face of his bigotry. "I am his kind. His sister, actually."

His eyes met my face and I saw a sneer as he raked his eyes over me from top to bottom again. Maybe disgust? Apparently, adoption wasn't something he approved of. At least adoption by "not your kind" wasn't his gig.

Well, fuck him. Dash was my brother whether we shared anything genetic or not.

"He's a dragon. He belongs with a pack." This came from the woman who stood behind the doughboy and I remembered the visit from Adak.

These three were all dragon shifters instead of the strange mix of myths that had come calling earlier, but something about this group had me on even higher alert than I'd been on with Adak and his sidekicks. This guy felt all ... wrong.

The doughboy held up a hand to silence her and graced me with a smile that made my skin crawl. "We'll give her time to realize that. I'm sure she'll come around to our way of think-ing." And when he said the next, his tone left no doubt of his salacious message. "And when her brother joins Heritage Pack, I'm sure we can find a … place for her."

Yeah, full body shudder at that one.

Heritage Pack had the ring of originalists to it. Bigoted believers in returning to the old ways, before the Goddess Lilliera changed the world. Before she gave myths a human form to balance their myth form. Originalists wanted the old ways back, and usually that meant they wanted humans to be nothing more than chattel or entertainment for myths.

And I had three carloads of these assholes in my driveway.

Backup came in the form of Adak as he stepped out of the woods to my right.

"I don't think she wants your help, Gransen," Adak said, his voice a low rumble and almost deadly quiet, like he was confident enough not to have to raise his voice. Confident that his message would get across without it.

I caught the scent of a campfire on a hot summer night as Adak stepped close to me, taking up a position on my right flank, all bulging muscles and walking sexual fantasy. If I had any time for sex right now, I might dwell on those muscles.

He didn't step between me and the threat. His position was one of support not the kind of domineering protection that assumed I couldn't take care of myself.

As Adak and I glared daggers at the other dragons, I wondered what Adak's beef with them was. Getting between myths fighting over territory could be messy and this had that sort of stink to it.

I filed away the names Gransen and Heritage Pack for the future. I would find out more about them when I wasn't facing them down as they tried to take my brother from me.

I saw a tick in Gransen's jaw as he gave what he seemed to think would look like a nonchalant shrug—it didn't.

"Sure. No biggie." He turned his eyes to me. "Keep in touch.

Your brother's going to need our help sooner rather than later. None of us wants him to suffer."

The way he said brother reiterated his feelings for my relationship with Dash and I took a step closer, my eyes holding his.

Adak stayed where he was as the others got in their vehicles and pulled up the rutted drive that would take them back to the paved road.

When he pulled his attention from the others and turned to me, I shifted to look at those gold eyes.

He seemed like the kind of guy who would always step in to protect others. Being a guardian was part of his nature.

"You realize he won't let a human into his pack? Heritage Pack is all about species purity and myth dominance."

I couldn't stop the laughter that lit my eyes. "Didn't you hear? He'll find a place for me." I put the emphasis on place just as Gransen had.

I thought I heard a deep growl in Adak's chest but he cut it off. "You need to be careful if Gransen's got an interest in you and your brother. He's not someone you want to mess with."

"And do you have humans in your pack?"

"Family is family."

I believed him. There was something unsaid there. Something about the value of family.

Based on what I'd seen of his pack, he didn't share Gransen's belief in species purity. Adak had witches, dragons, and wolves in his pack. But would that really extend to a human?

Not that it mattered. I couldn't join his pack, even if Dash went that route.

He lifted a paper bag. "I was dropping off valerian root tea."

I eyed the bag not wanting to know what the tea cost. Still, if he said it would help Dash, I'd cut into our food budget for it. I could eat light. Wouldn't be the first time.

I reached into the leather pocket strapped to my thigh and pulled out my wallet. "How much?"

His face went blank and he shook his head. "Nothing. Our coven members grow it on our property. You're welcome to it." He pushed the bag closer, holding it practically under my nose.

I watched him, thinking of the implications of that statement. To grow anything but the hardiest of crops meant they had to have a strong coven capable of working earth and air magics equally. It took power to detect magic burns when they began and even more strength to work the earth and air in ways that could protect crops until the burn subsided.

Accepting would mean we owed this man. I wasn't okay with that. I pulled a fifty-dollar bill out of my wallet. It was half of what I'd budgeted for groceries for the next few days, but I'd have to juggle. "Will this cover it?"

Adak gave me that single brow raise I'd always wanted to be able to do. I practiced the damned thing in the mirror when I was little and never did get it. Damn him.

He took the bill. "Sure. That covers it."

I nodded, took the bag, and turned to the porch.

"How is he?" he called from behind as my feet hit the front steps.

"Fine," I said, not bothering to turn around or expand. He hadn't needed to bring the tea, so what was his deal? Was it protecting the little guy or did he have an ulterior motive for wanting my brother to join his pack?

Gransen had shown up out of nowhere to try to bring Dash into his pack. Adding a new dragon to their ranks would strengthen them, sure, but did these two packs see more in Dash? Did they sense he was special and want to use him the way the Illieri would?

I reached to the sheath on the side of my hip, the one where the leather had split just enough on one side to let me slip a finger in and slide it along the blade.

I didn't flinch as I drew the droplet of blood I would need to get through the ward. As I put my hand on the doorknob, I thought of something.

When I turned, I found him scenting the air and knew he'd caught the scent of blood. You couldn't hide that from myths.

"Hey, do you know anything about a hedge witch named Vivian?"

Adak tilted his head. "Powerful with illusions. Not much else. She has friends in high places, though. She and a vampire named Dominica run a club down in Gransen's territory called Illusion. People who come to the club can buy a glamour from Vivian for the night. They can look like anyone they choose to."

He shrugged a shoulder like he didn't understand the desire to look like someone else, and I guess he wouldn't. What would he need with an illusion looking the way he did?

I filed the information on Vivian away.

"Is this Dominica part of a fury?"

Adak shook his head before asking a question of his own. "What do you need with Vivian?"

"Heard she's hiring for a job."

He nodded, but it was slow and the gesture seemed to say he was thinking about something. Evaluating.

"She plays games. Works with some shady people. Watch yourself with her."

"Will she pay me when the job is done?"

"Yeah. If she says she'll pay you, she will, but taking work as an unregistered dagger isn't safe here."

I would ask him about goats, but he seemed like he was going to lecture me about not being licensed. I didn't need that.

I slipped my hand back to the doorknob letting it suck the droplet of blood from my finger. The weight of Adak's gaze stayed on my back as I walked inside and shut the door.

As much as I wanted to, I didn't let myself look through the window to watch his ass as he walked away. I went to the kitchen and pulled out a small soup pan in lieu of a teapot and ran water into it. If this valerian root was going to help Dash, I was going to get it into him right away.

A small slip of paper was attached to the bag with a phone number and the words Nova Force on it. I slipped it into my pocket and pulled a chipped cup from a cabinet.

I almost dropped the cup two minutes later when I turned and found Dash leaning in the doorway of the kitchen.

"Shit." I shook the splash of hot tea off my hand, cursing the burn as much as the loss of a few drops of the fifty-dollar tea.

"What are you doing out of bed?" I set the tea on the table and then tucked my body under his arm to help him as he moved to sit.

He laid nervous eyes on me. "The fever broke."

We might not know much about what was happening to him, but we did know what that meant. When the fever breaks on a dragon going through their first shift, it meant the shift would happen in the next twenty-four to forty-eight hours, assuming his shift was going to go normally.

It meant he'd have a small reprieve from the pain for the next day or so and then it would come back with a vengeance. From the little we knew, the pain he would suffer in the coming days would be like nothing he'd faced so far.

I put the tea in front of him and ran a hand through his loose curls. His fever breaking meant I didn't have a whole lot of time to decide on a pack. So far I'd met two of them. I needed to find out if there were any more in Austin to consider.

And then it would be decision time.

"I have to run out about a job. You'll be alright here for a while?"

Dash smirked and raised his cup of tea. "Never better."

If only it were true.

7

Roxie

Hunt hadn't been joking about the Christmas trees. There were at least thirty of them on the front lawn of the deep purple house. She'd decorated them, too. With black ornaments.

It was an interesting choice.

"Hunt sent me."

The words were blunt, but they got the job done. Vivian the hedge witch pushed the door open and jerked her head into the space behind it in apparent invitation.

I kept one eye on her, one on the interior of the house, and a hand on my knife as I entered.

The woman wore flowing black skirts and a blouse that looked like it was once lavender but could use a good wash. Or a blow torch. A blow torch might work just fine.

Her appearance said she was in her sixties or seventies, but since she was a hedge witch, her age could be anywhere from twenty to a few centuries. Powerful hedge witches could create illusions that were hard to see through and sometimes used those to alter their appearance.

This one seemed to be going for the mother crone look. If the mother crone never bathed. I could feel some power coming off her and Adak had said she was strong when it came to illusions. A hedge witch couldn't attain that sort of strength without some seasoned years behind them. That and blood sacrifice. I didn't like this woman.

When she moved further into the house, down a hall, and into a kitchen, I followed, studying her. She didn't move like she was older than thirty or forty, so I had to wonder if the whole thing was an act. In fact, she didn't smell like she never bathed, so maybe the dirty clothes and grime under her nails were part of the illusion.

I said it before and I'll say it again. Hedge witches were crazy as fuck.

She sat at a round wooden table with crystals of various colors and sizes in front of her.

I didn't sit.

"Hunt said you have a job." I wasn't exactly being polite, but I didn't like hedge witches overmuch. There was something parasitic about their very nature that bothered me.

She shuffled the crystals around on the table, stopping to rub one here or there. "Do you know anything about vampires and zombies?"

"I wouldn't be very good at my job if I didn't."

She studied me and I wondered if she had plans to test me the same way Hunt had. Not that she looked like she could put up that kind of fight.

She squinted her eyes at me, rubbing another of the crystals. "Ever run into an indie with a zombie?"

There were vampires who lived independently, outside of any fury or affiliation. Most people called them indies. I'd known of a few who kept a zombie for a time on their own and

I'd once met a very powerful vampire who kept two that she would walk around on chains wherever she went, but she was an exception.

"I have."

She nodded and looked back to her crystals, pushing them around again, rearranging their order. She moved some to touch each other, others she set apart at precise intervals.

All myths left small trails of magic in the world, some shedding more than others. Hedge witches collected that magic like leeches and used it to fuel their spells. I knew hedge witches could use crystals to pull magic from the universe, but she'd be disappointed if she was trying to get anything off me.

I was Illieri by heritage, but I'd never come into my magic, leaving me essentially human.

"You must be desperate to work off the books."

I raised my brows but said nothing. What was with people here? Was every dagger in Austin registered?

She lifted a shoulder. "Not my problem."

At least she was smart enough to know that much. "What's the job?"

Rheumy eyes met mine and she licked her lips, the gesture creepy in so many damned ways.

"I'll have to bind you before we talk about the job."

The practice was standard, but I never liked the ritual. She pulled a small knife from somewhere in the folds of her skirt, but I shook my head, pulling my own dagger.

She gave another careless shrug and pulled a candle out, lighting it and placing it in the necessary holder. A binding plate was easy to get ahold of nowadays, but I stepped in, examining the candle holder in the center of the plate and the runes etched in the edge to be sure they were right.

Not that she couldn't cast an illusion to make this look like a standard binding plate when she was actually binding me to something else, but if she did that I'd just beat her senseless until she released me.

Well, fuck. Now I'd taken my head down a whole fucking rabbit hole of possibilities. My tongue ran its pattern over my top teeth.

How badly did I want this work? Pretty fucking badly, to be honest.

I nicked the edge of my hand with my knife and let the blood drip over the candle as I read off the incantation. "Bind these words to me alone, price for sharing paid in bone."

It was a simple incantation but it worked. If I talked about what she wanted me to do, I'd lose a body part for that slip.

She gave a nod and set the plate at the center of the table. Anything we discussed would be covered by the oath until the candle was extinguished by the hedge witch.

"There's an indie vampire that lives to the west of here a ways. Dominica Ruiz. She's not associated with any fury but she's keeping a zombie. I want you to take out her zombie. She doesn't have near enough control over him."

I snorted. "You don't think she has enough control so you're just going to order his death?"

Not that I was all about fighting for zombie rights or anything, but it seemed a little fucked up of her to act like judge, jury, and executioner. Although she was asking me to take on that last part.

Did she know about Hunt's brother? Did he know she'd order his brother's death if she didn't deem Hunt strong enough to maintain control of him?

Then again, I'd never seen anyone with as much control over a zombie as Hunt had over his brother. It suggested his brother still had some level of brain function, something I'd never seen or heard of. They weren't called mindless killing machines for nothing.

I'd killed a rogue zombie once that had been terrorizing a

city on the west coast where Dash and I lived for a year, but a zombie who was under a vampire's control was a different matter. Vampires were fast, powerful, and deadly. Zombies even more so. I'd have to take out both of them since one wouldn't stand there while I killed the other.

I rubbed my forehead.

The hedge witch gave an indelicate snort. "A dagger with scruples? You have a problem with killing a zombie? If I told you it mauled a child last week? Is the killing of a child reason enough?"

Why yes. The killing of a child would be enough for me to act, but I wasn't going to take her word for it. "Where and when?"

She seemed to size me up for another minute before pulling a slip of paper from deep in the folds of her skirt and handing it to me.

"Prove it, if you must, before you take him out, but my price is his head."

"You want the head?" Good Goddess, this woman was nuts.

She waved a careless hand. "It's an expression. I'll know when the job is done."

I looked down and found a name and address on it. *Jake Connors.*

8

I WENT DIRECTLY to the address on the paper, pulling over at the curb and looking around the run-down neighborhood as I cut the engine. The remnants of police tape blew in the wind from their positions tied to old fence posts that no longer held a fence. As soon as I opened the car, the scent caught me and I held still, breathing deep to get it all.

Engine oil, the wretched scent of aging blood, and something else underneath it all. Something woodsy and earthy, which didn't at all seem to fit the neighborhood. I didn't have the ability to smell in the way a myth could, but I'd been trained to pay attention to what my nose could pick up.

The smells were wrong for a zombie attack. The scent of zombie would linger for days if one had been here and I wasn't picking up on that at all.

I walked over to the lawn where it happened. The newspaper story I dug up showed a shot of the lawn, a small body covered with a pale green blanket, blood seeping through in a gruesome testament to the violence that had taken place.

The body and blanket were gone, but the blood remained and a small amount of brain matter that made me cringe.

I felt the person come up behind me before they spoke. I turned my head, keeping my body loose in case I needed to move to defend myself.

It was an old man, maybe in his sixties. Possibly older. He leaned heavily on a wooden cane. "You a reporter?"

I looked down at myself. I was wearing my usual. Leather pants, a strappy tank top, shit kicker boots with wine colored roses painted on them, and my sheaths strapped to every available part of my body stocked with daggers and stakes.

I looked back at him with a gesture of my hand to my clothing. "Really?"

He scratched at the thin hair on the top of his head. "Have to ask. We've had too many damned reporters poking around here. They all want to talk to the family. Brutal bastards."

I crossed my arms and frowned at the grass again. "Were you here when the boy was attacked?"

"No one was," the man said, apparently deciding he could answer my questions even though I'd offered no explanation for them. "Happened in the middle of the night. People heard screaming, came running, but whoever did it was gone."

If a vampire had good control of their zombie, they could get them in and out quickly for a hit like this. A rogue zombie was different. They wouldn't kill and run. They would wander around until they found another live meal on their buffet table of life.

He pointed to the grass. "The boy was there. Pajamas torn and bloody."

It was hard not to picture someone else there. Dash might be my brother, not my child, but we'd been on our own since he was five. I'd raised him. I couldn't imagine what those parents must have felt. When they went to bed, their child was safe, alive. They woke to a nightmare.

I shoved the feelings back and focused on getting information. "He was the only one hurt?"

The old man nodded, a single jerky movement and I saw him swipe at his cheek with the back of his hand.

"No one saw anything?"

"No one. A ghost. Gone."

I nodded my thanks as the man walked away, and then stepped closer to the grass, inhaling a deep breath again.

Not a single sign of the death stench zombies carried with them wherever they went.

I glanced around before rubbing my hand over the grass and raising it to my nose.

Yes, there was the reek of decaying blood and I could make out the rot of the brain matter that had been left, but zombies had more to them than that. I couldn't describe it. There was another layer to their odor. Maybe it was the twist of the magic gone bad when what should have turned them into a vampire began eating them from the inside out instead.

Whatever it was, it meant this scene had been made to look like a zombie had killed the Connors boy, but it hadn't.

It also meant this Vivian lady had set me up to think that same thing. I didn't like being set up and I wasn't the kind of person to walk away from that without finding out what the hell was going on.

9

Adak

I WAS AVOIDING Lesande and Tag, but if there was a right way to do it, I'd found it. I went to the take-out window at Home Slice and picked up five slices of the daily special—sausage and pepperoni—and sat under a tree to eat it.

I hadn't offered to buy the property from the warrior and her brother.

Probably because seeing Gransen there on her land made me see red.

I'd gone through three of the slices before I calmed enough to taste what I was eating. Which was a damned shame since the tomato and cheese mixing with the spice of the meats wasn't something I wanted to miss.

Home Slice bought its produce from our pack so unlike most places in town, they had fresh ingredients and they knew what to do with them.

On my fourth slice, I calmed down enough to see that the Gransen excuse was a bullshit one. I had other reasons that I hadn't made the offer and they weren't ones I fully understood yet.

I pulled out my phone and messaged Tag and Lesande. *Going to bring the fledgling and the warrior into the pack.*

As I waited, I started on my last slice of pizza, thinking about getting a few more. I should have just bought a pie to begin with.

Lesande was the first. *A human?*

Tag replied before I could. *The boy feels powerful. Might be worth it.*

I wasn't going to debate the issue with them. I shut my phone off and finished my pizza before grabbing three more slices and a dozen pepperoni rolls.

Tag was right. I'd felt power coming from the kid, but it was more than that. Combining our packs to form Nova Force had been a decision about power and strength. The ability to protect the dragons of my pack more than I'd be able to if we were a traditional pack.

I had no idea why I'd come to the decision to add these two —and that alone had me on edge—but I had the feeling bringing them into Nova Force was the right one for the pack. The move that would bring the most safety to my people in the long run.

What I couldn't say for sure, though, was whether I was making that decision because I thought having them on our side was better than having them against us someday or not.

There was something about the pair that was different. I should push the unknown away but my gut told me, that would be a mistake. One with potentially fatal consequences.

10

THE SCREAMS HIT me before I was even out of the car. I slammed it into park and cut the engine, boots hitting the gravel lot and running flat out for the cabin.

The ward wasn't broken—both a good and a bad thing. Good because it meant there wasn't anyone in there with Dash, but bad because I had to stop and prick my finger to get through it.

He was seizing on the floor of his room, half on the bed half off, when I got to him.

I called out to him as I pulled his head onto my lap, but of course, he didn't respond.

When I got done swearing the proverbial blue streak, I calmed my voice to a more soothing tone and brushed the hair from his eyes.

"You'll get through this, Dash. I promise, I'll get you through this."

We should have had more time. We were supposed to have

a day or more after his fever broke, but he was different. I should have known we couldn't count on that.

What were these seizures doing to him? What about the temperature? He felt hot enough that I had to think this could be doing permanent damage to him. A body was only made to take so much. Could a dragon body take this kind of heat?

And what about an eggborn dragon? There was always that extra layer to worry about with him.

I was going to have to take a chance on one of the dragon packs in the area. I cradled Dash in my arms as I ran through what little I knew about our choices.

Heritage Pack was out of the question. My gut was telling me to stay as far away from Gransen and his pack as possible, and there was no way in hell I wanted Dash mixed up with originalists. Not that he'd fit in with them. I'd raised Dash right. He was no bigot.

Nova Force was our only other option, but I wouldn't make this choice based on that alone. Adak had helped us when he didn't have to. I thought of the time he'd come with the witch and wolf shifter in the beginning. None of them had looked cranked up on Vamp Dust or anything like that.

I didn't understand how their pack worked with different species in it, but the fact they could all make that work had to mean something. Shit, Dash and I were different species and Adak understood we were family no matter the difference between us.

Adak had brought tea to help Dash when he didn't have to. He'd asked how he was, not demanded to see him. I could see Hunt was right. Adak was a good leader. And Lord knew he was powerful. Dash would need that, too.

Nova Force it was.

11

I DIDN'T WAIT to be invited into the mansion of a log cabin that must be Nova Force's main stronghold. Adak caught up to my side, taking my arm to steer me to the right down a long hall. I allowed the hold as we entered what looked like a mini hospital in two large rooms connected by a set of glass doors. Dash was in a bed, being held down by two strong men as he writhed and screamed.

And then his body jerked, and he was seizing. A cushiony Black woman with braids running down her back spoke to Adak. "He needs the pack bond."

I looked at Adak. "You'll take him?" I'd already asked him back at the cabin, but I asked again.

He held my gaze for several beats before giving a nod. "If that's what he wants."

He crossed to Dash and spoke to him, his mouth close to Dash's ear. I don't know how my brother processed anything through the pain, but he nodded, wild eyes on Adak.

Something in me broke as I watched Dash bind himself to a new family, but I shoved the pieces aside. I'd deal with them later.

Dash needed this and if there was one thing I knew in life, it was that I would always do what was right for Dash.

Adak spoke several words and Dash whispered something back to him I couldn't make out. I saw something happen. I don't know what. Some swirl of magic. Some connection.

It was done.

The doctor moved back to Dash's bedside with several of the other dragons stepping up alongside her.

Adak put a hand on my arm, warm and strong. "He'll be fine. Our dragons will take on some of his pain. It will be better for him now."

"Tell me how that works." Alpha or not, no way was I just letting him do whatever he wanted to my brother without explaining things.

Adak raised a brow but answered. "Dragons are naturally able to take on a bit of one another's pain as packmates, but our coven uses magic to amp up that ability tenfold. If we divide the pain among enough of us, it's negligible to everyone. He won't have seizures. He'll just wait the shift out in relative ease, and we'll take him outside when he's ready to turn."

I looked at my watch again as if it could offer a countdown to Dash's shift.

When I looked back, I found gold eyes watching me with some measure of amusement. At least one of us was having fun.

"We can wait down the hall if you'd like," he said, gesturing toward the door. It was an offer but there was that alpha sternness to it that said I should listen.

I had half a mind not to, only for the sake of showing him he couldn't direct my movements, but I wanted to grill him for as much information as I could. Letting him think he was leading this dance might help.

I checked on Dash again, finding he'd stilled as the other dragons and the healer stood around him. He really did look like he was napping now.

Adak led the way down the hall to the other end of the sprawling home to a large room with couches. There was a fireplace on one wall so large I could have stood in it without crouching.

Adak sat on one couch, stretching his legs in front of him, one ankle crossed over the other.

I leaned a hip on the arm of another couch and tilted me head at the big man. "How does your pack work? I've never seen a pack with dragons, shifters, and witches in it."

In fact, I'd never seen anything like the place he'd led us to in the fold of magic that housed their pack. Trees that seemed to too old for where they stood in northwest Austin filled the area.

Visitors to the pack lands came through the woods and out into an enormous open field with the cabin on steroids at the left end of it. A creek ran behind the house and beyond that, I'd seen fields of crops, a vegetable garden, and livestock.

It was a proper village with the mansion-sized cabin in the center and smaller homes out past the crops and dotted through the surrounding woods.

There were no cars in sight, which made sense since there wasn't a road into the fold and many of its members could fly. I did see a couple of large pieces of farming machinery and would bet those came in on the back of a dragon.

"That's why we call ourselves a force instead of a pack." Adak leaned back, throwing one arm over the back of the couch like he didn't have a care in the world. Or maybe he was just trying to politely counter some of the tension I was leaking from my pores. "We're technically two packs and a coven, but we've chosen to live together in a force." He lifted a shoulder. "But, yeah, it's essentially a pack."

"And you're its leader."

He tilted his head in assent. "I am."

That made no sense. "The alpha of the shifter pack and the leader of the witch coven have, what? Signed their power over to you?"

His grin was slow. If he minded me digging into how his pack worked, he didn't show it. I had the distinct feeling, though, that if I asked something he really didn't want to share, I'd never get a word out of him. No one was going to make this mountain of a man do something he didn't want to do.

Could I seduce it out of him? Would I mind the effort? Not likely.

"They are my seconds, my advisors, but yes. They've agreed to abide by the decisions I make in the best interest of the force. Of course, as with any good pack, the authority of the alpha is freely given and can be taken away. If I'm not acting in the best interests of the force, they'd walk."

"That simple?" I asked.

"That simple."

Now for the not-so-simple question. "Do your pack members have family members outside the pack?"

He was quiet for a minute. "The pack is our family. Some people have extended family in another state that's not part of the pack, but," he glanced away, "for the most part, pack is family and family is pack."

"Except me." It wasn't a question.

"Will you join us?"

I had the sense he didn't know what to do with me, but he would make the offer out of familial obligation.

That was okay. I didn't need his pity offer. "I can't do that."

"Why is that?" Now he was the one who was tense. I didn't imagine the hint of insult in his tone.

I faced him head on as I answered. "My one and only job in this world is to take care of Dash. To keep him safe. I can't do that if I'm not free to make decisions the way I see fit. I'm guessing if I join your pack, I lose that freedom."

Again with the little head tilt. "True. You would have to agree to honor the decisions your alpha makes."

I'd expected him to point out that I was no longer needed as Dash's protector since he and the pack would now have Dash's back. He didn't and I was glad.

I couldn't explain to him that there was no way I could trust him and the pack to stick by Dash when the Illieri caught up to us someday. That day was inevitable and when they came, they would bring death to any who stood between them and Dash.

When the time came, I would stand for Dash, even if it that meant giving my life.

I laughed. "Who would be my alpha? I don't exactly fit into any of your groups."

His narrowed eyes told me exactly who my alpha would be. I'd answer to him.

I let the smile fall. "I can't do that, Adak."

He knew my reasoning. "What makes you think your brother needs your protection? He's a dragon, Roxie."

I wasn't ready for that conversation yet. In time, I would tell him what Dash was and about the Illieri, but I needed to be sure of him first.

He nodded and stood. "Very well. I welcome you here as our guest until your brother settles in with us. After that, you'll need permission to enter our lands to visit."

His words weren't meant to be cruel, but they cut deep, opening a bleeding gash in my chest that would likely never heal. They emphasized the loss I was about to face. Underscored the fact that I couldn't turn back. For better or worse, Dash had a pack now. And I was on the outside.

Adak stilled like he was listening to something before meeting my eyes. "Time to get this youngling outside and see what kind of dragon we have."

"Huh?"

He pointed to the side of his neck where a small, tattooed circle of runes sat just below and behind his ear. "Comm spell. Tag says it's go-time."

Adak and I turned and ran as one, triple-timing it down the hall. I'd have to ask what the hell he meant by comm spell later.

When we drew close to a door marked infirmary, he put on a burst of speed and moved ahead of me into the room. He was back in front of me before I reached the door, Dash in his arms like he weighed nothing. My brother writhed but didn't seem to be in pain.

I followed Adak as he wound through a series of hallways I hadn't seen yet, stepping out onto the back side of the house's wrap-around porch. I took in the twenty or so people standing around waiting for us and my tongue raked its path over my teeth as I held my arms loose by my sides, ready to draw my daggers if this went south.

Much as I couldn't wait to see Dash transform for the first time, I knew if he was drastically different from all of them—if there was something that marked him as egg-born, as other—they might turn on him.

I didn't care how many there were or how big they were. I'd be ready if they did.

Adak set Dash down on the grass and stepped back. He came to stand by my side, stopping me with a hand on my arm when I made to move forward.

"He needs room. He'll be all right now. The pain will be short. It's almost over, Roxie."

He was wrong. It already was. It would never again be Dash and me against the world. He belonged to them now.

12

I STARED, heart pounding as bronze light began to swirl around Dash. This was it. My brother's first change.

"You did it, my warrior," my mother's voice said inside my head.

The bronze mixed with copper and gold and I heard gasps in the crowd. Was he different than them?

I had to fight not to charge in, weapons drawn, to stand over him in case they turned against him.

My fingers tapped the hilts of my daggers and I skimmed the onlookers, watching for anything that seemed out of place. Any hint at what they were thinking.

For a brief moment, Dash seemed to be in pain. Then he was there, his dragon form emerging from the colored mist. The being before me was incredible. Stunning.

Dash was enormous, larger even than Adak. His rough scales didn't lie flat and sleek as Adak's had when he was in dragon form. My brother's scales were thick and domed, black turning to brown on his sides and then a burnished bronze on his belly. He had plates protruding from his spine running from the back of his head to the tip of his tail. He looked ferocious.

The clearing was utterly still and I knew then he was different. He didn't look like they expected him to look, and that was bad.

He was larger than even Adak—by at least a head, and since that head was a dragon's that meant more than a yard. He turned his face to me and opened his eyes. Brilliant cerulean blue like gemstones among the scales.

No one moved.

I took a step forward, ready with my blades should they turn on him.

And then he winked at me. The little pisser winked at me.

The tension broke and the crowd laughed at the antics of their newest member.

Adak moved past me and vaulted, still in his human form, climbing straight up Dash's back. His feet found purchase as he climbed, taking careful hold of one of Dash's plates to settle near his head.

I remembered Dash watching Bob the Builder episodes when he was young. Bob would casually hop on one of the bulldozers and hang off it, coffee cup in hand, as it drove him where he needed to go. The image flashed in my mind as I looked at Adak, steady and sure on my brother's shoulder.

"Okay, big guy. In a minute, you're going to feel an uncontrollable urge to cough. I want you to turn that way." Adak gestured, pointing toward a break between the trees.

That's when I realized the group had split, leaving an opening where the trees separated.

Adak kept talking. "It's not going to hurt you, so don't panic, but in a minute, you'll have flames coming out of that giant block head of yours. We don't want you to take out any bystanders. Or the house. Or the woods."

I had to hand it to Adak. The way he stayed so steady and almost joked with Dash through this made me calmer. I had a feeling it had the same effect on Dash.

Then I felt the heat as a roar of molten lava shot from Dash's mouth.

And I do mean molten lava. This wasn't flame. It wasn't normal.

They might have aimed Dash at a break in the trees, but it wasn't enough. Nova Force members dodged out of the way as the trees on the edge of the opening went up in flames. The crowd shouted, several witches moving into action and dousing the flames with water and air spells.

I moved, pulling a knife in either hand, putting myself in front of Dash. There were a lot of them and only one of me, but that lava Dash just breathed should give them pause. I was banking on it to help me get us out of there.

They didn't come at us, though. None of them.

They were laughing.

"He's incredible!" A teenage girl with blonde hair smiled at me and I recognized her as the witch who'd ridden Adak's shoulder that first day. Aster, I remembered.

Even though he was different, they didn't seem worried about it. They were celebrating him.

"Pretty amazing to see, huh?" she asked.

I watched Dash.

"All right, big guy," Adak said. "Let's take these wings of yours out for a spin."

Dash raised his head and swung it back toward Adak.

Adak patted Dash's thick neck. "You won't drop me. But even if you do, I'll just shift. No biggie." He pointed to a tall witch with spiky blonde hair who oozed power and confidence. "Lesande is an air witch. She's going to build you a ladder to climb. Just get those feet up the ladder and shove off. Move those wings of yours, Dashiell. You're ready to fly."

My eyes flicked to Adak when he used Dash's full name and he met my gaze, challenge in his own. He was showing me Dash had shared his full name with him, that he was Dash's family now.

Then Dash was moving and I didn't have time to sit in my feelings.

Pride hit me full on again as I watched Dash begin to move his feet the way I'd seen Adak do, like he was climbing steps in the air in front of him. That's how they took off without launching from a height. The air witch was creating a ladder out of thin air for him.

I held my position as the downdraft from Dash's wings plowed into me. I saw Dash wobble in the air but heard Adak shout words of encouragement to him.

The others were cheering him on, all of them seemingly as happy about the addition to their ranks as any proud parents might be.

Several of the dragons joined him, shifting and taking to the skies with him. A few of the witches and wolves jumped to their spots on the dragons' shoulders.

Aster stayed by my side, probably out of pity since I wasn't able to join the sky party.

"He's an earth dragon?" What I really wanted to know was did she see what I saw? Did she realize he was too big? That there was something about him that said he held power and strength he shouldn't at this age.

"Yes," she said with a wide smile. "They're wonderful. Incredible, really. I've never seen one that could breathe lava like that, but some earth dragons manipulate sand and dirt like an air dragon can make tornadoes."

I looked over and saw a beaming look of awe on the face beside me.

The woman's gaze stayed on Dash as she spoke again. "He's large. Beautiful."

Well, hell. Was that a teenage crush or an assessment?

I looked at those who had stayed on the ground. No one looked panicked. Maybe they all thought he was just big for his age. Here's hoping they kept that view.

"Are you an earth witch?" I asked Aster. Most witches and dragons had an affinity to one of the elements: earth, air, water, or fire. Unlike wolf shifters, who were all linked to the earth.

She shook her head. "My strength lies in manipulating the winds." With a little wave of her hands, she stirred the leaves on a nearby tree.

An air witch, then. I wondered if the coven were all air witches since they seemed to use them to help the dragons launch from the ground.

Then again, based on the fields of crops I'd seen growing out back, they had to have earth witches as well.

"Lesande is my mother," she said, pride evident. "She's one of the strongest air witches there is."

She pointed to the witch who'd built the air staircase for Dash. Lesande stood, hands on hips and head tilted back, assessing Dash. I couldn't read her expression, but I knew she was one I would need to watch as she judged my brother.

I tore my gaze from the pack and looked up at Dash. He had shifted. We'd done it. We had survived. He was one step closer to fulfilling his destiny.

13

WHEN DASH finally made it down out of the sky, the pack herded us into the building for dinner. I hadn't thought through the fact that we'd be eating and sleeping here for a few days.

Eating with the pack. Somehow, I pictured the wolves tearing into raw meat, the dragons swallowing sheep or pigs whole, and the witches stirring a brew over a cauldron.

Yeah, so I was stereotyping.

And I was wrong.

Dinner took place in a large hall with three long rows of heavy wooden tables. The chairs and benches that faced the tables looked like they were hand carved and polished and I wondered how long the pack had made their home here.

The tables made me think of the big farm table at the cabin I'd been pretending carried a heritage of family for Dash and I. Only these ones looked legit. I could tell they belonged to this pack. That they held its history.

One of the witches showed us to a pair of seats at the center table and I was surprised to see Adak sitting across from us. I would have thought he'd have Tag and Lesande near him at some head table for the three leaders, but I saw Tag across at another table and Lesande was down at the end of the table we sat at.

I let the scents of the room fill me and my mouth watered. Plates of braised vegetables and roasted meats circulated as people talked and piled their plates with food.

I put a slice of meat with a brown sauce over it on my plate and passed the plate over to Dash. He rolled his eyes at me and scooped a portion about three times the size of mine onto his plate.

I passed the next few platters along without taking any and watched as he piled his plate high. The roll he'd stuck on the edge fell onto the table. He picked it up and put it in his mouth as he tried to add mashed potatoes, having to put them on top of some roasted veggie thing to make it all fit.

I pushed the pot roast around on my plate and squirmed in my seat. The extravagance of the meal made me uneasy.

"Is something wrong with the food, Roxie?"

When I looked up at Adak's question, I realized the people around us were all watching me. I glowered at him in answer, but Dash was cracking up next to me lessening the effect of my glare. I shot him a look and he laughed harder, still shoveling mashed potatoes into his mouth. So much for my pseudo mom superpowers. The kid had truly flown the coop.

Adak looked around. "We have plenty. Take as much as you want."

"I'm fine, thank you." I lifted my fork and knife.

Adak pushed a bowl of salad my way. "Are you vegetarian? We've got salad."

I had noticed the salad. It wasn't the kinds of lettuce that were more likely to withstand a magic burn. There wasn't a shred of the uber thick romaine/kale blend bred to withstand the burns in there.

This looked like soft, buttery baby leaves. And slices of red onion and cucumber. Bite sized tomatoes cut in two.

Whatever they were doing to protect their crops from the burn, it was effective. If humans could see this, there would probably be another war.

Most scientists agreed the magical burns were a result of the increased magical population on the planet now that myths were living in the open and reproducing freely instead of hiding in the shadows.

A lot of humans were pissed about it. They saw the burns as the myths' fault. Knowing myths were eating like this would push this shit right over the edge.

By now, the whole room was watching the exchange.

Always the helpful teenager, Dash offered his armchair psychologist theory. "Enjoying food makes Roxie feel guilty."

Dash put on his best Mom/drill sergeant imitation, "Eat what you need to be nourished and get back on that field. We aren't finished training for the day."

Enough of this. "She wasn't wrong. Food is for refueling not enjoying."

If things had been quiet before, they were basically mausoleum-silent now.

"She usually just opens a can of beans for lunch or dinner," Dash said. "And breakfast is dry cereal or an oat bar. It's really sad."

All the hard looks I was shooting at him bounced off. Little brothers were a pain in the ass. Dash was addicted to cherry slushies. He'd never really taken to Mom's way of thinking about food, but then again, he didn't train as hard as Mom and I did. He knew he'd have the power of his dragon form behind him someday and dragons could pretty well burn off whatever they ate.

"And the only way she serves our meat is to cut it up and cook it on the stove in a pan. Never grills or barbecues it or anything. No seasoning, or nothing."

I rolled my eyes at Dash.

Adak leaned across the table and looked me in the eyes in that way that made me think those golden orbs were only seeing me in that moment. That the whole rest of the room had vanished somehow.

Sexy as fuck, in case you're wondering.

"Do me a favor, Roxie, take a bite of that pot roast."

I grumbled something about alphas wanting to control too many damned things around them.

"You know you want to," Dash taunted, not realizing how much the eyes all around me made me want to retch. Or throw a knife at someone.

I lifted my knife and fork again, but Adak spoke.

"You don't need that," he said and reached over with his own fork using the side of it to cut a piece of the pot roast for me. The damned meat looked like it might melt and I wasn't the least bit surprised even the food jumped to do his bidding.

When Adak reached over, holding the fork out for me, I drew a line in the sand and took the fork out of his hand.

I wasn't about to let this man feed me in front of his whole fucking pack.

Freaking dragons and their control.

All thoughts about snark and controlling the fork left my head when I put that first bite in my mouth. Gravy smothered the perfectly seasoned meat and I might have whimpered if I was alone.

I swallowed it down and forced my face to stay clear. "It's good, thanks."

Adak's laugh was low and deep and too damned knowing.

I added a shrug. "Really, it's not bad."

Now he was roaring with laughter and he wasn't the only one. Dash and the woman on my left side started filling my plate with as much food as Dash's.

I should insist on serving my damned self, but I didn't. I took another bite of the pot roast and didn't seem to have the ability to fight. Flavors burst across my tongue and I sighed. It was the good kind of sigh.

"Just because you need food for energy, doesn't mean you can't enjoy how it tastes," Adak said.

I didn't answer. I was too busy trying the other things on my plate while Dash continued to share all kinds of inappropriate things with the members of Nova Force.

I picked up a roll and broke it open to find steam coming out. It was crusty on the outside and soft on the inside.

Dash was acting like I'd never tasted good food before. I had.

Okay, but really, it was nothing like this. Nothing at all. We didn't have the time or the money to eat like this.

Dash was on a roll. "She eats hotdogs cold. And canned meat."

I heard a universal gasp at that one. Everyone knew canned meat was never what it said it was on the label nowadays, but it got me protein on the cheap when I needed it.

I didn't care what Dash was saying because I was attacking chips with some kind of melted cheese concoction on it.

"Queso," Adak said with a nod to the cheese as the rest of the room started asking Dash about my eating habits.

"When she's in a hurry, she just cracks eggs right into her mouth and eats 'em raw."

They all had varying degrees of "eww" or "gross" to that one.

Okay, I was starting to mind. I turned to my brother ready to light into his scrawny ass, but Adak reached across the table and put another roll in my hand.

The man was not fighting fair.

An hour later, my stomach looked five months pregnant with all the food I'd eaten and I was really hoping we were safe here because I could barely stand, much less defend us if I needed to. Yet another way I knew our mom had been right about indulging where food was concerned.

The pack's main house was quiet now, and Dash and I sat on a small patch of the roof outside the window of the guest room they'd given me. I bumped his shoulder with my own, a move I hadn't made since he'd started getting sick at the start of his first shift. It was good to have him back. He turned soft brown eyes on me and smiled.

Adak hadn't said when I had to leave but I figured I'd stay a couple of days. I was normally a rip-off-the-bandage kind of girl so even staying for that long seemed like putting off the inevitable. But Dash asked me to stay for a bit, so I would.

Some of the force were out patrolling the city, although I was still a little unclear what they patrolled for. After his lesson with Adak, Dash had shifted back into human form with the help of a few of the dragons talking him through it. He seemed exhausted to me, but he insisted he was too keyed up to sleep.

I put my finger to the tattoo behind his ear. It matched Adak's.

He fingered it himself. It was fully healed so I knew it had been put there with magic, not the traditional means.

"Communication spell from the witches. Lets the pack members talk to each other in our heads. Telepathy or something."

"Can they listen in?" I asked, on edge at the thought of any kind of spell like that on my brother.

He shook his head. "No. I have to activate it. I think about who I want to speak with and touch it to activate it and when I speak in my head, they hear it."

I looked out at the pack lands that surrounded us. There were the woods and the main building where we were, but there were also small cottages dotting the woods and fields of crops behind us. I could hear what I was pretty sure were cows in the distance, so they had to have cattle here, too.

"Crazy, huh?" he asked me, and I snorted my response.

"Ya think?"

We'd been saying much the same thing for the last hour, still marveling over the fact he'd finally shifted into his dragon form, but now Dash grew quiet.

"Rox?"

"Yeah?"

He stared down at the ground beneath us, before glancing over at me. "Are we gonna be okay? I mean, you and me? Are we okay now that I'm in a pack? Do you think you'll still—"

I turned and pulled his shoulders around to face me. I felt a pang at the insecurity he must be feeling. He might be fifteen, but with the way we'd had to live on our own for much of his life, it was hard to remember that sometimes. He really was just a kid.

And what he'd just gone through had to be hitting him hard. Adak had said there were all kinds of hormones flooding Dash's body from the change. It could be a really hard time, he said, but things would even out in a few days.

"Dashiell, we will always be okay, you and me. I love you and nothing will ever change that. Not belonging to a pack. Not living apart. Not even a few scales and that crazy hot lava breath you've got going on now." I waved my hand in front of my nose like I was waving away stink breath.

He laughed like I'd hoped for, and I pulled him in tight for a hug. He might be a powerful shifter, but he was still my baby brother. Still the little guy who used to pull my hair and try to trick me into eating worms.

We laid back on the roof and looked up at the sky, pointing out stars and making up constellations. And I soaked in the time with my brother. For a little while at least, we were safe here.

14

I STEPPED out onto the front porch of the lair—as I'd now learned the pack called the main house—my eyes going to the sky to pick out Dash among the other young dragons. Three days had passed as I ate and visited with the pack. I had run off the six breakfast tacos I ate that morning before showering and changing into fresh jeans and a lacy tank top.

Yes, I'd found out Texans made tacos into a breakfast thing, and I was fully on board with it. Fully.

I kept my eyes on the sky. There were three dragons, two shifters, and Aster out on the quad at the front of the lair. As I watched, the dragons swooped low to allow the others to drop to the ground before circling and letting them hop back on, climbing high into the air with them on board.

I'd never get tired of watching Dash in his dragon form. It was incredible to see him spin on his side and twist in the air like he was swimming in the sky.

Not only was he majestic as he maneuvered with increasing

grace and ease, seeing the others shift mid leap onto the dragons' backs was, well, magical. There was no other way to
describe it.

The wolf shifters that rode on the dragons were incredibly
powerful, being able to make that shift so quickly.

I hadn't witnessed Adak shift again in the time we'd been
here, but I wanted to. A lot more than I'd like to admit. Where
Aster had magic and beauty when she shifted from her human
form to her witch form, he was pure power. Strength like I'd
never seen.

I'd heard a couple of the other teenagers in the pack talking
about Dash's size and power in his dragon form, but it seemed
like teen envy not the rumblings of him being off in some way.

Dash landed in the field setting down startlingly softly for
such a large body. I kept expecting to feel the earth shudder
underneath the dragons with every landing, but they managed
to cushion it just right somehow.

Vikram, the young wolf shifter who'd been riding on Dash's
shoulder, leapt from his back, shifting as he dropped for a deft
landing on two human feet.

Dash, still in dragon form, swung toward me and lowered
his giant head. The others were all making their way back to
the lair, presumably to get ready for lunch. Meals here
continued to be an event with tables laden high with all kinds
of meats and vegetables. I'd never seen so much food in my life.

As the field fell quiet around us as the others left, Dash
nudged me and flicked his head back toward his shoulder.

I laughed and shook my head. "No way, little man."

He snorted, hot dragon breath showing his displeasure at
the old nickname and nudged me again. This time, he lowered
his front shoulder and waited. Even in his dragon form, I could
see the challenge in his eye. The look that said he dared me to
climb on.

Hell, what was I thinking? I would be nuts not to do this.

Who doesn't spend their whole life wanting to fly? And for the first time in years, I wasn't alone in the world with no one to protect my brother if something happened to me. I wasn't the only thing standing between him and Isle if she found him.

For once, I could do stupid. I could do fun. He now had an entire pack, a family, looking out for him.

I stepped forward and climbed onto him the way I'd seen Adak do the other day, bouldering higher and using his scales for purchase. I grabbed hold of the large scale that poked out at the base of his skull and planted my legs wide on his back.

I realized we had no way to lift off since there wasn't an air witch around to build a ladder for him. I looked around. They'd all gone in to eat.

Dash seemed to have a way around it. I held on as he took off galloping toward a ten-foot-wide tree that stood at the end of one side of the clearing. It wasn't a tree that should have grown in this area, but there it was. Someone had chopped off the top and stripped it of its branches and leaves, but despite that there was no sign of rot.

I'd noticed it before and wondered what it was for. I got my answer as Dash leapt toward it, spun to hit it with his back legs and used the momentum to thrust himself up into the air.

Apparently, Nova Force had more than one way for their dragons to achieve lift off.

And with that, he took flight, skimming just over the grass at first, as my breath caught in my throat. As we neared the edge of the trees, he swooped up, banking left to turn in a wide circle, moving higher as I whooped in his ear.

Nothing in the world could compare with this feeling. Nothing.

Every worry I'd had left me. Everything that had weighed on me for months was gone with the first swish of his wings, the first gust of cold air across my cheeks.

I searched for the emotion I felt as we soared above the

clouds. Joy. It was sheer joy. I wasn't sure I'd ever felt that, but once I knew what it was it hit me full force in the chest.

"Higher!" I shouted, not at all sure he could hear me above the wind. I wanted more of this. I wanted to keep flying and never come down.

As he banked into another turn, he climbed, taking us above the tree line. It looked as though I could reach out and touch the clouds, or step right off him into a billowy bed of poofy white. I knew better. We weren't really that close to the clouds, but the feeling was heady.

I closed my eyes and focused on the feelings. The quiet. The utter lightness I felt.

I didn't see what made Dash bank suddenly, but I felt it. Felt the movement and heard him grunt, almost as though he wanted to swear but couldn't in this form.

Then there was a flash of dragons on our right and I knew we'd almost collided with someone coming through the fold in their dragon form.

I didn't hear or see much after that. Just the heat of panic, flashes of sky as I lost my grip, plunging into nothingness. My throat closed and my breath seized in my lungs as I grabbed for something, anything, but there was nothing for my hands to cling to.

I was free-falling toward the ground. Toward a very hard and very deadly landing.

Dash bore down on me from above, trying to get to me in time.

I braced.

Even if he reached me, with the speed of the fall and his inability to finesse those razor-sharp talons, he would split me in half. Shredded.

Panic marred his face and I didn't want to see it there. Didn't want to face his fear, his realization that he'd dropped me and couldn't reach me in time.

I closed my eyes. The rush of the air no longer felt freeing. It didn't feel calming. I felt nothing but the sheer terror of knowing I couldn't survive this fall. I screamed then, despair and terror and panic erupting from me.

Then came anger and rage as I realized after all we'd been through, I was about to die from a dumb ass flying accident. A fall from my brother's back.

I wouldn't die this way. Couldn't. It couldn't come to this.

I sucked in a breath. I was out of time. If I didn't stop this fall, I was going to die. *No!*

15

Roxie

My stomach slammed to a stop a full three seconds after my body did. I had to fight not to throw up as Dash struggled to halt his descent before he hit me.

I heard shouting. Someone calling for Lesande as heavy footsteps raced at us. A thud as Dash veered to the side, slamming into the ground next to me instead of the usual graceful landing.

Adak running at us, all but shooting fire at me with his eyes as he skidded to a stop and glared at me and Dash.

I didn't know who the hell had caught me, but I owed them.

Problem was, they didn't put me down. I was stuck hanging in the air. Dash shifted before racing to my side.

Adak stewed, his anger palpable.

"Shit, Rox, Shit!" Dash stopped and put his hands out as I floated in the air. "I'm so sorry, Rox."

Lesande took only a moment to join the group, her eyes assessing as she watched me float.

"Not to sound ungrateful for the catch, but can whoever has me put me down?" I looked around and realized the dragons who'd almost crashed into us didn't have air witches with them. They must have been out flying alone not patrolling with weres and witches on their backs.

If they hadn't stopped me, who the hell had?

It was Lesande who answered, but the look on her face was a bit disconcerting.

"Roxie," Lesande said, "picture your body coming to a landing gently, two feet hitting the ground to stand up."

I looked at her like she'd lost her mind. "Excuse me?"

"Put yourself down, dear."

I stared for what seemed like several minutes before trying it. I didn't manage the soft and steady landing she'd described. Instead, I fell on my ass onto the grass with an indelicate "ummph." I rolled in a flip and came up to my feet, saving myself from further humiliation.

Eyes locked on mine, Adak spoke. "With me. Now." He pointed at Dash without looking at him. "You and I will talk later."

I had the distinct feeling he was hauling me into the principal's office, but I wanted answers as much as he did, so I didn't argue. I followed Adak and Lesande through what had become a crowd of onlookers. I was pretty sure the whole force was there, piled onto the porch and spilling out onto the lawn.

And I heard the whispers as I stepped through the path Adak forged.

"Who stopped her?"

"It wasn't Lesande. She didn't make it out here in time."

"It wasn't me. I was eating lunch."

"Who was out here?"

We left the voices behind and went into a room I hadn't seen before. It was obvious it was Adak's office when he shut the door and settled in behind the mahogany slab serving as a desk.

When he opened his mouth, his words were anything but calm.

Sure, they were steady, controlled, his voice quiet. But it was the deadly kind of quiet. The kind a truly scary person goes to right before they take your head or stake you. The kind that said run.

"Do you have any idea why our wolves don't ride on dragons without a witch?"

I didn't answer him. I didn't need to be lectured by the man. I already knew what we'd done was stupid, but I sure as hell wouldn't explain myself to him.

A low rumbling growl sounded as he clenched his fists and gnashed his teeth at me.

"You don't ride a dragon without my permission!" he shouted. "Ever!"

Oh no.

Oh, no he didn't.

I stepped closer to him, putting my hands on the desk and matching his scowl. Why the hell was he getting all fucking fire breathy with me?

"Did you really just try to give me an order, alpha?" I was pissed and I wasn't afraid to let him know. "I'm not your pack. You sure as hell don't get to tell me what to do!"

"When you're on my lands, I do!" Adak growled again, this time washing the room with a wave of his alpha power.

I didn't back down, though from the look on his face, he'd expected me to.

Lesande stepped up to us. "There's a more important topic here, Adak."

She was still eyeing me and I didn't at all like the look.

The glare never left Adak's face but he turned his head toward the coven leader.

She spoke to me, not him. "Roxie, I made it to the porch in time to see you stop falling. Only you, me, and Dash were out there when you stopped. I was about to spell the air to catch you, but I didn't. There were no other air witches out there or anyone else who could have stopped your fall."

Adak's face went hard as he turned to me. It was no longer anger. It was something more. Something truly lethal.

"What the hell are you hiding, woman?"

In the face of that, I laughed. Should I have? Oh hell no.

But really? They'd lost their minds if they thought I'd saved myself out there.

Okay, so the laughter might have bordered on the hysterical, but I'd just dropped from a height of I-don't-want-to-think-how-high and I'd somehow survived.

If you asked me, I was entitled to a little hysteria. I realized my hands were shaking and I moved back and let myself sink into a chair, running my tongue over the back of my teeth.

When I'd managed to clench the shakes out of my hands, I looked up to find them both watching me. Hell, they were probably trying to figure out if they needed to get a shrink in here to handle the crazy lady.

Did the pack have shrinks on hand?

I couldn't explain to them how I knew I had no magic to do what Lesande was describing. It wasn't just a matter of saying, "The only magic I have is the Black girl kind."

Gee, Adak, I'm descended from a long line of warriors beholden to the Goddess Lilliera. We're her warriors on earth, waiting to serve her on the day she returns to this realm. Every Illieri warrior is granted magical powers when she comes of age, but I never got mine because Mom kidnapped a dragon egg so he could save the world someday and we've been on the run ever since.

Yeah, there was no way I could explain this to them without sharing the secrets Dash and I had guarded for years.

Lesande came and sat next to me on the couch, pulling a piece of chalk from her pocket.

"Will you try something for me, Roxie?"

I didn't expect this tone from Lesande. She was a leader, a drill sergeant. She didn't take time out for cuddles and kisses.

But right now, her tone was motherly patience. My little episode had seemingly brought out the mama in Lesande.

I raised my brows at her and waited.

She knelt on the floor in front of us and drew a small circle with several symbols along the inside edge of it. I recognized most of the symbols.

Witch children were taught to draw symbols and circles to manifest their magic. She was doing a kindergarten level spell, using the small circle in front of her as a magical container. The circle would contain the power she called on with the symbols. It looked like she was setting up a simple light spell.

When she had all but the final symbol in place, she handed the chalk to me and pointed to two sections of the working. "Close this line and this line."

I did as she directed, murmuring "abracadabra" dryly as I did. I could have sworn I heard a choked growl from Adak. Probably he was trying to reign in the urge to strangle me.

When nothing happened, I handed the chalk back to her.

She wiped the floor clean and started another circle, placing a sheet of paper from Adak's desk in the center of it. I recognized symbols related to air and guessed the spell would float the paper if it worked.

Again she handed me the chalk and pointed at a line to close.

"Ala kazam!" I looked up at her when nothing happened.

She tried again, this time with symbols I didn't recognize, moving faster now, handing me the chalk again.

"Hocus pocus," I said, this time with a lot less feeling as I closed the lines.

Nothing happened.

A fourth time, she drew a circle, and I would guess this one had something to do with water magic, the fourth element.

I was out of magical words, so I closed this one silently. Nothing.

I stood, brushing the chalk from my hands and shrugging at them. "Trust me, I didn't stop myself. Maybe one of your air witches saw me from a window or the woods or something and was able to act in time, but it sure as hell wasn't me."

Adak's eyes on me were grim. Lesande's wary.

I headed for the door. "I'm heading back to the cabin today." I turned back and my words were genuine. "Thank you for having me here while Dash adjusted. It means a lot to me to know he's with people who care for him, who've welcomed him as family."

Adak gave only a slight nod, his eyes still watching me like he might be able to decipher me if he only looked hard enough.

I nodded and turned to walk out. It was time for me to let Dash get on with being a member of the pack. Time for me to let my brother grow.

16

Dash convinced me to stay for dinner, and really, how was I supposed to resist that? Nova Force knew how to eat. Tonight's theme was barbeque. They introduced me to ribs where the meat falls off the bone when you pick it up. There was also corn bread with jalapenos in it and greens cooked with ham hocks.

I remembered eating like that one other time when we were kids and Mom brought us to a local church of the Goddess Lilliera, where they were having a cookout. A woman with braids that hung down her back—braids I was jealous of then and still was now—smiled as she handed me a plate of white bread, greens, and meat.

Mom scowled but let me and Dash eat it while she went to look for her contact in the group.

I never knew why Mom was meeting the man, but he gave her some money and we left. I suspected she did a job for him. Back then, I was only nine and Mom didn't take me on jobs with her.

She started taking me a couple of years later, and that's when I found out mom's jobs often involved putting a stake in a vamp's heart or tracking the more deadly myths no one else wanted to hunt. It was how she made the kind of money to buy us the houses on the safehouse list we'd been working our way through all these years.

But at that cookout, I hadn't known any of that and I was happy to be sitting side-by-side with other kids, even if they looked at us a little funny. My skin was brown like theirs. Dash was white as hell, though, and one girl asked why he didn't match us.

I wanted to punch her in the mouth for that, but that would draw attention. We didn't draw attention to ourselves. I could protect him better by sticking worms in her backpack when she wasn't looking.

Which I did.

Dash hadn't been old enough to understand the question then, and I was glad for that. He'd been happy gnawing on a chicken wing.

The barbeque served up at Nova Force rivaled that of the church cookout and I'd watched him put away a dozen wings on top of the plate of ribs we shared.

Tag, Adak's right hand, slid onto the seat next to me. They were all making the rounds feeling me out and I guess it was his turn.

Not that he addressed me or anything. Not so much as a nod.

As he tore into the brisket on his plate, I noticed scars running up and down his arms. It took a lot to scar a shifter, especially one with a coven of witches at his beck and call the way they had here.

I didn't stare, though. I knew what it was like to feel like people were analyzing your every move. I reached for another roll and a slab of butter. Who knew hot buttered rolls could taste like heaven in your mouth?

"Shouldn't you be grilling me by now?" I asked after Tag didn't start a conversation.

He grunted. "Eating."

I had to chuckle at that. The man was after my heart with that attitude.

At this point, I was working on seconds. Someone put a bowl of coleslaw in my hands and I scooped some and passed it on to Tag. He didn't take any before passing it and I looked around to see most of the wolves didn't take any of the sides. They seemed all about the meat.

Made sense, I guessed.

"Why Austin?" Tag asked.

I hadn't realized he'd slowed his eating. He hadn't stopped, mind you, but he wasn't shoveling it in anymore.

I went with something close to the truth. "Our family has a cabin here. Makes sense for us to use it."

"It sat empty for a long time."

"It did."

He didn't roll his eyes at me, but he was giving off that kind of vibe. The vibe that called bullshit to my non-answers.

I studied him. He was probably only in his thirties, same as Adak. They were both young to be in control of such a large pack. I wondered how many wolves were under his authority. I'd seen dozens of them around.

"How many myths are there in Nova Force?"

He didn't seem to mind the question. "One hundred and eighty-two," he said, and I choked on the sip of water I'd just taken. It was more than I'd expected.

He went on. "Fifty-eight wolf shifters, sixty-one witches, and sixty-three dragons, including our newest member," he said tipping his head toward Dash who was talking to Aster across from us.

"Is that why Adak is the pack leader? Because there are more dragons than weres or witches?"

Tag pushed his plate away and leaned his elbows on the table as he watched me. "He's the alpha because he's the most powerful of us and makes good decisions for the benefit of the Force."

From what I'd seen, Tag and Lesande seemed to act almost as Adak's betas, but I'd heard them referred to as the other alphas by Adak, so he seemed to acknowledge their status.

Tag turned the tables on me quickly. "Who do you think caught you when you fell?"

I honestly couldn't tell if he was asking because he really wanted my guess or if it was a challenge. Maybe he was trying to tell me he thought I'd stopped myself like Lesande and Adak did.

Shit, for all I knew, Adak was using that comm spell to feed these lines to Tag and grill me through another mouthpiece hoping I might slip up and say something different this time.

"Any of the sixty-one witches in the force, I guess." I thought about that and corrected my statement. "Any of the air witches, anyway."

He nodded, slowly, and my sense of him was that he was a guy who was never going to rush into judgment on something. I could see why his wolves would follow him, even when he'd pledged himself and his pack in this odd arrangement Nova Force had.

He shoved back from the table and left without another word and I had the urge to call out and ask what he'd decided.

Did he believe me? Did he have any idea who'd caught me?

And would he keep asking questions till he got answers the way I expected Adak would? Questions were never a good thing in my world.

"The witches are dancing," said Kai as he walked by us a few minutes later while I cleared my plates, handing the dirty dishes off to a woman who was stacking them in a rack I guessed would go through an industrial dishwasher.

Aster grinned at me and Dash, putting herself between us so she could loop one arm in either of ours and pull us along.

"Come on, the more people we get dancing, the more magic we can build," she said.

I knew witches could regenerate their magic with dancing but I'd never seen it. It sounded like she wanted us to be part of it and I sure as hell hadn't ever done that.

Most covens I'd met were secretive. They wouldn't let nonmembers into their rituals even if it did mean being able to generate more magic.

I guess it was different in the little commune these people had going.

The only thing was, I didn't dance. I was piss poor at it. Dash couldn't either. He looked like a rubber band that had been thumbtacked to the floor when he danced, his feet stuck to the floor while he wiggled his body around like rubber.

I didn't know if he even realized how bad he was, but he never seemed to care.

Maybe I should be glad they weren't having an orgy and asking us to join in. Sex was another way for witches to build power. That could get awkward if you asked outsiders to join.

"Come on," Aster squealed as she tugged at us, then let go of our hands and went spinning into the circle of dancers. Dash followed her looking at me like I was crazy when I didn't follow him.

I didn't bother with an excuse. I just crossed my arms and watched from the side, daring anyone to try to get me out there. Wasn't happening.

"What the hell is that?" I couldn't help the words slipping out of my mouth as I stared at a teenager who was gyrating like he was Elvis up on stage.

My answer came from a deep voice next to me. "That's

Declan. He's pretty convinced all the women want him now that he's hit sixteen. He's also pretty sure that move is going to get him a witch in his bed tonight."

I looked and saw the man next to me rub a hand over his face before tipping his head back and whispering, "Goddess, help me," to the sky.

I looked back to the boy. "You responsible for that?"

He sighed. "He's my brother."

I nodded. I knew how that was.

The man put out his hand in greeting and I turned to look at him then. I wasn't sure I'd seen him around the place yet. He had creamy tan skin and long eyelashes and those big loose curls most women would kill for.

I took the offered hand.

"Darius Starke," he said.

Good Lord, did everyone here have superhero sounding names? Adak, Lesande, Tag, Darius? Where was a Bob or Leslie when you needed one?

"I'm Roxie."

He laughed at that. "I know who you are. Everyone does."

"That's not good," I said, and I meant it.

My stomach clenched. I'd just learned this pack was a lot larger than I thought it was and I didn't like the idea of standing out. I should be blending in, going unnoticed, but I guess Dash and I hadn't done a very good job of that since we got into town.

He shook his head. "Don't be so worried. I'm the pack's enforcer. It's my job to know who and what everyone is." He turned to me now, dead on, and I got the full impact of his stare. It wasn't a light stare. "My alpha tells me you're not what you say you are. You smell human to me, but Adak is never wrong. He and Lesande say you're not human."

Darius was still holding onto my hand. I could pull it away and put some space between us with a nice little push kick to his chest, but that probably wouldn't ingratiate me to Dash's new pack.

Instead, I met his eyes and held that suddenly hard stare. I could see why this man was the pack's enforcer. He was a dragon, though I couldn't tell what kind. Still, it didn't matter what kind he was with the size he had in his human form. He must be six feet four inches and all muscle. His dragon form was likely formidable as well.

But more, it was the way he'd gone from being all buddy, buddy "I have little brother problems, too," one minute to the cold hard stare of a man who would protect his pack at all costs the next.

So Adak had talked to him and Tag about this crazy idea I'd caught myself in that free fall. Who else had he talked to?

I didn't like them all thinking I was something other than what I was. An Illieri warrior with no magic was for all intents and purposes human. Period.

My mom was Adira the Righteous, Wrath of Lilliera. She was meant to sit at the Goddess's right hand someday, but that didn't change facts. Illieri were all born with no magic. It was only granted to us by the Goddess herself through trials and ceremonies when we came of age.

But I didn't explain any of that. I held his hand firm and I held his gaze and I waited him out.

With whiplash like speed, Darius switched back to the hapless big brother routine with a shrug and turned back to the fire. "Damn, that boy."

I looked where he was looking and saw his brother Declan was still gyrating his hips.

Well, at least Dash wasn't the worst dancer out there. There was that.

Dash and Aster had joined Declan. There was more than just the glow of the firelight in the air. There was a glow around all of the witches. There were so many of them and so many people dancing that the magic was thick on the air.

Before the Dawning and even after it as myths fought through the Dawn Wars, they would have hidden, dancing in small groups inside homes in basements or out in the woods so no one would see this.

I wandered away from the fire to where a small group of children sat listening to one of the women I'd met earlier tell a story.

Brenda, I think her name was. She was heavyset with round cheeks and deep brown eyes to match her afro of hair. Her cheeks almost glowed and I wondered why she wasn't dancing with the other witches.

A man sat next to her, tan and kind of Nordic looking with the kind of looks that could have made him a model. The smile on his face was the same as those of the kids surrounding her. He clapped when she said something and she smiled indulgently at him.

She was telling the story of our creation and I listened, curious to know what they taught their children. Mom had always scared the crap out of me and Dash when she told us about the Goddesses that created all myths and the humans. Mom's version was flush with details about the wars that took place after the Goddess Dabria created her vampires and zombies. How they hunted the other myths and tormented humans, using them as chattel to feed their deadly cravings. How the myths and humans turned against each other instead of working together.

Brenda smiled at the children as she leaned in close. The man next to her mimicked her, leaning in, too.

"Evalyne was the sweetest of the Goddesses," she said, "but she loved many gods and many loved her, giving her children by the hundreds. Though she loved her children all dearly, she didn't have enough magic to share with them. The humans she birthed were plentiful but had no magic."

I leaned my shoulder against a tree and watched the faces of the children as they listened. They were smiling, eyes wide. What would it have been like to grow up in a pack like this? Is this what life would have been like if we'd stayed with the Illieri?

I didn't remember much from my childhood with them. I'd been five when we left and I thought maybe I should remember more, but there was really nothing more than fuzzy blank pages when I tried to look back on those days.

"Lilliera was the most powerful of the Goddesses, strong and wise with a heart to match. She lay with only the most powerful of the gods and gave birth to the myths: the witches and dragons and wolves. The trolls and dwarves." Brenda scanned the children. "The unicorns and fairies. Pixies and sirens. All were given robust magic from their mother Goddess."

"Till the bad one came," said one little boy.

Brenda looked to him, humor creasing her face at his exuberance before affecting a dramatic tone for the next part of the tale. "Dabria lay with no one, for fear if she let anyone close to her they would steal her power. She was angry when she saw the children of her sisters and wanted children of her own."

"So she made them," shouted the boy, a delighted wicked cackle following. "They're the abominations."

The man next to Brenda clapped again.

I pressed my lips together to keep from laughing. He was loving this. Him and the little boy, both.

"She did," Brenda said. "She gave her blood to humans, warping their nature and vampires and zombies were born. The fighting began and humans and myths turned against one another as Dabria's progeny spread her evil."

This was starting to sound a lot more like Mom's version.

Brenda's smile returned and I knew she was going to turn it away from the war. Not something Mom had done. Mom had never sugar-coated things for us. She said we needed to know the truth of it all to face what was coming.

"Lilliera saw that her children and Evalyne's children were suffering. She even felt for the children of her evil sister and wanted to act to save them all. But it would take an enormous sacrifice."

"She sacrificed all her power!" the boy yelled and a girl next to him shushed him angrily.

Brenda looked unfazed. "She did. She used all of her power to save them and to lock her sisters and her away from the realm of their children so the fighting would subside."

The boy leaned in, bouncing excitedly. "And the myths were all given a human form and told to hide and live apart. The humans lost their memory of the myths and the abominations. The vampires and zombies were crippled by the sunlight."

The kids were all talking now, all trying to put in their own bits and pieces of the story. How the myths kept their power and magic but dwindled in numbers because they had to hide. How the vampires couldn't come out in the daytime and could die from a stake to the heart. How humans were made to forgot.

"Why did the Dawning happen?" one girl asked.

It was the little boy who answered. "Because they're coming back! The Goddesses are coming back!"

Brenda's face grew tight but she brushed off his response. "Because the Goddesses willed it and it was so," was all she said.

Dash hadn't been born until after the Dawning and I was only four when it happened. I don't remember much of the day the world woke up to the universal knowledge that the myths and legends of their childhood were real and had been living among humans this whole time.

Mom said it was surreal to see the humans figure out the

awareness they suddenly had wasn't an insane dream. That their neighbors and friends all knew the same things they suddenly knew. That myths were real. That shifters and witches lived among them. That vampires weren't the thing of legends.

And most importantly, that humans were not the strongest, smartest, fastest bad asses at the top of the food chain.

I always pictured people walking out onto their front steps and looking at their neighbors for signs of "otherness." Like, that one has a big nose and I once saw her pet a cat so she must be a witch. Or that one always eats her meat rare and she once said she loved the full moon so she's got to be a wolf shifter.

Of course, the fighting began almost immediately. Humans thought they could exterminate the myths like they were bugs invading their planet.

The saddest part was that humans rarely targeted myths in those early attacks. They were piss poor at telling the difference between a human and a myth so they went around attacking and killing other humans most of the time.

Myths ended up coming out of hiding when they realized humans would continue to die if they didn't do something to stop it. That led to the Dawn Wars, but that's a story for another day.

There were a lot of theories out there on why the Dawning happened. Some said the Goddesses were returning and the Dawning was to prepare us. Some said they believed Lilliera's magic simply couldn't hold the binding on the humans' minds forever.

The effects of the sun and stakes on vampires seemed to be solid, though, so who knew?

I walked away from the group and looked around again at the lair in the distance, at the houses and cabins, the animals and fields of grain and vegetables. Dash had found a good place. If he had any shot of being safe from Isle and the Illieri, of having a good life that didn't involve constant fear and running, this was it.

We'd done it.

What, now, did that leave for me to do? I took a deep breath and let it out slowly.

I would wait and I would train. I would watch from the outside. And if Isle found us—when Isle found us—I would finish her before she could ever get to Dash and his new family.

I would finish what my mother had started, for good.

17

Roxie

It was full dark when I got back to the cabin and only the quiet greeted me. I crept through the silence to the kitchen thinking that maybe I should get a dog or a cat.

I missed Ghost. When he first started visiting our place in Colorado, he'd been a puppy with the big belly and off-balance gait that went with that. I'd watched him grow into an adolescent pit bull, with a beautiful gray coat and round eyes that alternated between making me crack up at his antics and melt into them like they were bottomless puddles.

I blew out a breath. A new dog wouldn't be Ghost. Not to mention, there were days I might be out on a job nearly twenty-four-seven. If Dash hadn't been old enough to make a bowl of cereal for himself when we lost our mom, that kid would have been hungry a lot.

I stared into the kitchen pantry. I wasn't hungry after that meal with Nova Force, but I needed to take stock and see what I had in the house for tomorrow. Not much. I had black beans, white beans, and green beans. Yum.

The snap of a twig outside was the first sound I heard, but feet on the front porch quickly followed.

The house's ward was still up so whoever it was shouldn't be able to enter the cabin. Technically, at least.

In reality, now that we'd started coming and going through the ward, it might have started breaking down. Someone powerful enough might be able to get through it.

I pulled a knife from the sheath at the small of my back and went to the front door just as someone banged on it with what sounded like a very large fist. I hadn't heard any cars so they must have come on foot or by wing.

"I'm not buying anything. Get the hell off my land." I really needed to put up some no trespassing signs. Or some piss the hell off signs.

I couldn't imagine what it would cost to buy a ward on the whole property and then maintain it since I'd be crossing it all the time, weakening the spell. One of the reasons the wards placed on the cabin had stayed in place so long was because no one had ever opened them. No one was crossing through them day in and day out the way I was now.

"It's Gransen Harcourt. Your brother's going to get real sick, real soon if you don't let us take him. It's time to stop messing around and let us help."

I raised my brows even though he couldn't see me. Harcourt seemed a little pretentious for the man I'd likened to a doll made of dough.

Knife in hand, I opened the front door.

"Thank you for your concern," I said putting what Mom always called 'a little extra nice' in my voice. That little extra nice was to tell people they could buzz off without really saying so. "Dash and I are doing just fine."

He narrowed his eyes at me and looked past me into the

cabin. I saw him take a slow deep breath through his nose, and he wasn't subtle about it either. Like he wanted to make sure I knew he could smell things I couldn't.

As before when he'd come calling, I saw a few of his pack materialize out of the woods beside the cabin to stand behind him. I wondered if there were others at the back door, ready to try to breach if he gave the word.

Shit, shit, and more shit. How was it that I'd been in town for less than a week and I was already on the crazy man's radar?

I didn't like this man. In my experience, myths who preached about purity of the species and all that crap were just like humans who spouted racial shit meant to keep some of us down while they rose to the top. Or at least let them have a scapegoat when they didn't rise to the top.

He finished scenting the air and met my gaze again, eyes dark and full of accusation. "He's gone."

I didn't bother to answer. "Was there something else you needed?"

His upper lip curled.

"There is." The words held a dark edge now and I guessed he was abandoning any effort at cordiality since it was clear I wasn't going to bend to his will.

Score one for me.

"You were sniffing around my part of town asking questions about a kid. You'll stay out of my territory from now on."

I snorted. "Not likely."

He didn't need to know I wasn't taking the case. The hedge witch, Vivian, was up to something trying to manipulate me and lie to get me on it. I didn't need to be involved in that shit.

But I sure as hell wasn't going to tell him that. Besides, I didn't know this town well enough to know when I was in his territory or stepping on his toes.

Gransen growled low and deep in his throat when I didn't bow down, heat floating through the air to me.

I didn't falter when he stepped into me.

"You're going to want to move," I warned, keeping my tone even. It was either my upbringing or stupidity. I didn't know which, but I didn't scare easy and if I did, I didn't show it.

He didn't move so I stepped into him this time. I was about done being polite.

"I'm gonna spell this out for you. You need to get off my property or I'll remove you and it won't be in one piece. Dragons are damned heavy. I'll probably have to take you out in chunks."

He laughed, long and hard and right in my face.

I laughed back. "Get a toothbrush."

He growled and lunged but I stepped back through the doorway and the ward lit him up, sending shards of electric magic through him from head to toe.

He wrenched himself loose, stumbling back to the porch.

That probably fried what was left of the ward. I'd need to spend money to refresh it. Fan-freaking-tastic.

One look at Gransen's face told me he was about to charge. The figures of his packmates racing toward us confirmed it.

I really didn't want this happening in my living room. What little furniture I had wouldn't make it through a fight with these guys. Not to mention, they could pin me down too easily in here.

I ducked and shot forward, going under his arm to take the fight behind him.

With at least three of his pack approaching—shit, make that four—I had to move fast.

One-on-one, I might be able to handle them but it would be a lot harder fighting all of them at once.

"Don't shift!" Gransen yelled at his henchmen, his tone making it clear he was playing with me. "She's new in town. Let's give her a chance at a fair fight."

Fair? He thought four-on-one was fair? Asshole.

To me, he said, "Come on, girlie. Let's see what you've got!"

He leaned back against the porch railing and crossed his arms like he was enjoying the show. I didn't have time to worry about his entertainment.

It looked like he was going to let his men do his fighting for him, but Mom taught me early on never to trust that someone would stay out of a fight. I had to keep my eye on him just in case.

I ran toward the guy closest to the tree line, hoping to create distance between me and Gransen. I didn't want him jumping in and surprising me from behind. I almost laughed as I pictured me and the goon running into each other headfirst and knocking each other out like the old cartoons, but that thought only lasted a split second. At the last minute I went low, sliding like a baseball player.

I curled one leg under the other, driving my straight leg into his ankles and sending him head over heels. His forward momentum added to his fall and his right arm ended up behind him in a position that said it was broken or dislocated.

The crunching sound and his scream confirmed the injury, but there were three more still coming and I couldn't risk this guy getting up again. So, I did my best impression of the kicker on a football team, using his head as the ball.

As the others closed in, I grabbed for a rock the size of a small melon and lifted it over sleeping beauty. Another crunching noise when it connected with his brain let me know he would never get up again.

I didn't feel sorry for him when it was me or him. In a me or the other guy scenario, it would always be me...or Dash.

Another guy was almost on top of me already with two more coming only seconds behind. I tried to uppercut as I stood, using my legs for power, but he moved his head to the left just enough to avoid it. At least I wasn't on the ground anymore.

This guy had some training. I could tell by his stance. He kept his weight on the balls of his feet and he stayed mobile rather than planted to one spot like some of these idiots did.

He avoided a crescent kick by leaning back just enough for my foot to come within an inch of his nose. He threw out a couple quick punches that I was able to block. I threw an elbow that only slightly connected as he twisted out of the way.

From the corner of my eye, I saw the other two hesitate. Good. Maybe they'd realized I had a lot more skill than they were used to dealing with in humans.

The dragon before me was matching me blow for blow. I was going to have to fight smarter than him if I was going to beat him. I threw a couple punches at less than full power and then put my weight onto my back leg and turned like I was afraid.

He moved to take advantage of the opportunity and I had him.

I palmed one of my knives and used his momentum to shove it up under his ribcage to his heart. He looked down at the knife sticking out of his gut. I lifted my knee to my chest and drove my foot forward, driving the knife further in. I watched as his eyes rolled to the sky and he fell backwards, unmoving.

Gransen didn't appreciate that I had killed two of his men.

"I tried to play fair," he shouted at me, "but it looks like you want to fight dirty."

He gave a slight nod of his head to his two remaining fighters. They looked at each other like kids whose dad just told them they were no longer grounded and could go outside and play.

Well shit.

I could have handled the two of them easily if they stayed in human form, but they started to shift. It wouldn't take long and

I didn't wait around to watch. I ran for the woods, looking over my shoulder as I went.

They were air dragons. Smaller than other dragons at about eight feet tall. Thank goodness for small mercies, but they still wouldn't be easy to take out.

Air dragons meant two things. They could breathe air so hot you might as well be standing in the path of a blow torch, and they could create tornadoes. I wasn't keen on dealing with either of those situations.

I passed the stump where I had been chopping wood days before and grabbed the axe sticking out of it. I stopped just long enough to turn and throw it at the closest one. He roared when it nailed his arm and dug in.

It didn't slow him down long enough. He shook it off, blood running from the wound and kept right on coming.

I hit the edge of the woods just before I felt the air heat around me and heard the crackle as trees caught fire in their path. I could only hope the dense brush of the woods would slow them down and allow me time to get away. At least in here they couldn't fly overhead and see where I was. I ran for all I was worth, lungs burning with the effort.

They kept coming. They were destroying my land, taking out trees with their breath and I was only barely staying out of the range of that hot air myself. Branches and thorns sliced into me, but I couldn't worry about that now. I tried to change directions and lose them, but it wasn't working. They weren't as fast through the woods as I was, but I hadn't escaped them yet either.

And then came the tornadoes.

My hair whipped around and flying debris pelted me as I ran. The wind almost knocked me off my feet a couple times. I stumbled, scraping my hand on the ground as I tried to right myself and keep moving.

Just as I would escape one wind tunnel, they would create

another. If I wasn't careful, it would pick me up and throw me who knows where. I needed to find cover, and I needed to find it fast.

I looked for anything I could hide behind or under to regroup. A fallen tree wouldn't be enough. Then I saw a rock formation that might be large enough to offer some cover. I dove behind the first big one and then climbed my way through some others, squeezing to get as deep inside the pile of boulders as I could.

I slipped on one of the rocks, banging my shin and biting back a curse. That was going to leave a mark. I couldn't hear anything over the blood pumping through my body and the wind screaming around me, but I looked through a small opening.

They slashed through the woods searching for me. I waited for them to come closer, opening a sheath on the side of my thigh that I rarely used. This one held my backup magic weapons. Not the bo staff I couldn't control—I had no clue where that went when it wasn't with me—and not the magicked sheath at my ankle that held the relics Mom and I had collected for when the Illieri caught up to us.

I pulled a spelled peach pit from the sheath and steadied my breathing while I waited for the dragons to come closer.

It wasn't a real peach pit. The small explosive spell only looked like the remnant of someone's lunch.

One of the dragons came close to me, but the other was still too far to be hit by the spell. Problem was, if I waited too long, the one coming toward me would be on me and I'd be trapped.

I could either toss the pit and then try to do some damage during the confusion that followed, or I could stay holed up and hope they gave up.

Hiding was never really my thing.

I cupped the peach pit in my hands and brought my hands

up to my lips, whispering the words that would prime the explosion.

Two more seconds.

One.

I tossed the pit, aiming for the space between the two dragons, hoping to stun or injure them both in some way.

As the pit blew, I launched myself from the boulder, coming down on the dragon closest to me with my boot.

The swoosh of wings told me I had dragons incoming. Fuck me, if they had more than a few coming, I was done.

The sky filled with dragons, but they weren't coming at me. They were coming for Gransen.

This was Nova Force.

18

Roxie

I watched as the two air dragons barreled out of there, Gransen following with Nova Force on them the whole way. That fight wasn't going to be pretty, but it looked like it wasn't going to happen over my land, which was good.

I rolled to the side and came up to my knees, groaning at ribs that had taken a brutal beating and pain in my shoulder. My head was spinning and I was pretty sure I might puke if I tried to stand up. Or maybe even just sitting here.

Yeah, puking seemed likely right now.

I lowered my head and focused on sucking in steadying breaths. I didn't want to know what I looked like. It would be a miracle if I could get the sticks and leaves out of my hair and you could damned well bet my lipstick was smudged.

I stilled and listened. There were a few people at least, back near my cabin.

Out front of my home, three witches stood over one of the

dragons I'd killed. A wolf shifter and a dragon stood at their backs, guarding them.

This was Nova Force, too.

The witches held out their hands, chanting as magic flames engulfed the body, turning it to dust. I looked to where I'd fought and killed the other one, but it was gone. They were taking care of the evidence for me.

The wolf and dragon turned when I limped from the woods, but I raised my hands out to show I wasn't coming at them with weapons and they relaxed, turning back to their guard duties.

One of the witches looked up at me, her face grim. "We're sorry we didn't get here faster for you. Gransen isn't usually so bold, attacking so close to us."

"Unless he's attacking us," one of the other witches amended.

The first witch nodded. "Are you injured? We can do a healing."

As much as I appreciated them taking care of the bodies, I wasn't going to accept more than I had to. I couldn't pay for the healing and I wasn't going to ask for what I couldn't pay for.

I shook my head, no. "Appreciate the cleanup, though."

Their expressions ranged from shocked to offended. Most people probably didn't turn down healing when it was offered. Especially a human.

They left, though, climbing onto the dragon before she took to the air, turning toward Nova Force's lands.

I was taking stock of my injuries and wondering if it would have made a difference in that fight if I could have called my bo on demand—what good was a bo staff really, when you're dealing with tornadoes?— when I heard the crunch of tires coming down the drive.

"Are you absolutely shitting me?" I might have screamed

that at the sky a bit louder than I should have but, damnit, the Goddesses just had to be screwing with me now.

When I saw the Austin Police Department SUV pull into the clearing in front of the cabin a few minutes later, I spit out a few of the more creative curses I knew.

Did I really want to know why Austin's so-called finest was on my doorstep?

I didn't have any experience with the Austin police department yet, but if it was anything like those I'd interacted with around the country, it would leave a lot to be desired.

Law enforcement was supposedly "integrated" nowadays with most of the big city forces employing both humans and myths. The thing was, everything I'd seen of these integrated forces had shown me they picked the least knowledgeable myths on the planet to recruit. I had once met an officer who was a cat shifter, only she'd never actually shifted into her cat. She'd grown up in a human family and, as she put it, "didn't think she needed to be a cat to be able to do her job well."

And no, technically, she didn't need to be a cat to do her job well. But she did need to be more than a myth trying with all her tits to be a human.

Plus, who wouldn't want to shift to a cat form if they could? I mean, didn't she ever want to try it as a kid?

The SUV came to a stop in the clearing and the driver's side door opened. I bit down on a grunt as I stood, taking a minute to steady myself. I was going to need a lot of band aids. I looked around me at the carnage. The bodies were gone but it was clear a battle had occurred.

The woman who stepped out of the SUV was tall with dark brown hair, almost black eyes, and olive skin. She had a no-nonsense kind of look about her, hair pulled back in a tight knot, uniform looking like she'd pressed it minutes before getting out of the car.

I looked down at myself. Yeah, I dressed to impress. My

jeans were torn at both knees and I looked like a confused bird had tried to build a nest on me. There were twigs and leaves everywhere.

I didn't want to risk her shooting my ass on top of the night I'd just had so I called out as I started walking toward her.

"Can I help you, officer?" I looked her over as she turned, noticed the way she turned her body to the side while her hand hovered over her service weapon.

She was carrying some fire power. She had her service weapon on her right hip, but she also had two wooden stakes strapped to her right thigh, another gun strapped to her left thigh and a knife on her calf. That was what I could see.

Post-Dawning police forces let officers carry whatever they saw fit with few restrictions. I'd seen everything short of a flame thrower or rocket launcher and it wouldn't surprise me if one of them pulled that shit one day.

"You the owner here?" the officer asked.

I gave a single nod.

"I'll need to see some identification."

I watched her. "Why is that?"

"Your neighbors just reported a tornado coming through here."

"Four or five of them, actually." I tried to count the number of times the dragons had sent the mini spirals at me, but I wasn't sure. I lost track when my head almost flew off.

She wasn't giving up. "Care to tell me what caused them?"

I gave her my best, "you must be an idiot," look. Austin wasn't exactly known for tornadoes so she had to know they came from an air dragon or two. Unless she was that ignorant where myths were concerned.

No, she had stakes sheathed at her waist. She wasn't a stranger to dealing with myths.

"Dragon attack," I said and started limping for my front door.

She let me pass and followed me up the steps but stopped short of the door even though I hobbled through it and into the cabin.

"Did you want to report this dragon attack?" She called out while I went to the kitchen and grabbed the first aid kit. It was a mundane kit, not a magic one, but it would have to do.

I let her wait on the front porch as I sank onto the living room couch and put the first aid kit on the coffee table.

I took one of my remaining knives from its sheath and slit the right leg of my pants so I could see the damage on that side. From the pain and the way the skin was pulling I had a feeling my injuries were bad.

"Ma'am?" she prompted.

"Huh?" I took out a bottle of cleaning solution and sprayed it on the wounds, letting the excess run to the floor. I was past caring about keeping the cabin clean for the moment.

"Did you want to file a report?"

"Nope."

There was plenty of disgust in her next words. "He'll keep doing it if no one fights back."

Now I looked up. "Oh, I fought back. I'm just not going to bother with a police report. What's the point?"

She looked away from me with resignation in her face. She knew as well as I did that filing a police report would get me nowhere. I wondered why she didn't up and move to one of the cities where law and order had won out. New York or Los Angeles. The council had established footholds there early on and they'd never ceded command.

The council was in Austin in name only, it seemed.

Hell, she could even have moved to one of the small towns where humans had forced myths out and lived in a little cocoon pretending none of this had ever happened. Utah had a lot of those spots and I'd heard it was pretty.

"Tell me what you know about Gransen Harcourt," I said,

shoving aside my musings about political forces and the state of the council.

She didn't crack a smile. "That's not usually the way things work. I'm here to ask you the questions."

I wasn't going to beg. "Okay, don't."

She sighed and moved to step over the threshold, then stopped midstride and looked at me as if looking for permission.

Gransen had zapped the rest of the ward when he crossed the front door. No point trying to keep her out now. I waved a hand at the couch and she came and took the other end of it.

"Officer Lorna Adams," she said as she sat but she didn't offer her hand.

"Hi, Officer Lorna Adams." I didn't bother putting a bandage on any of my cuts for now. I did pull a thick stack of transparent film dressings out of the case to take into the bathroom with me. I'd be covering some pretty large areas with them after my shower.

"So Gransen and his crew were here. I'm surprised he came this close to Nova Force's territory, but he's been expanding his empire as of late." She looked around. "How'd you get mixed up with Gransen?"

I didn't know what she thought she'd see. Like I'd have a "hey I'm a criminal!" poster on my wall.

"You're supposed to be telling me about him," I pointed out.

"That really isn't the way this works," she said again. Humor mixed with the exasperation in her voice. I had that effect on people.

She was either going to tell me or she wasn't. I wasn't going to stress over it.

She shook her head again. People did that around me a lot, too.

"Gransen thinks he owns the lower part of downtown and all of south Austin."

"Does he?" I asked.

Now it was her turn to shrug. "For the most part. He runs south Austin, Adak runs things up here. A vampire has control of East Austin. When they keep things in balance, it mostly works. When they don't...well, things can get ugly."

"Do you know anything about Jake Connors' death?" I don't know why I asked. I wasn't taking the case. Still, I needed to go have it out with Vivian and find out what the hell she'd been doing trying to suck me into something that wasn't what it seemed. Might as well find out all I could first.

This time, she snorted. "Who are you?"

"Roxie Andrews. Dagger-for-hire."

The radio on her shoulder crackled and I heard talking over it, but she turned it down as though she didn't need to respond to it. I guess if she was called out to my location for a tornado complaint, maybe she didn't need to.

"Someone hired you to look into the Connors case?"

I understood her surprise. Daggers could investigate crimes that the police hadn't been able to solve, but the Connors kid had lived in a poor area. It was unlikely the parents could afford to hire a dagger.

"Pro bono," I said. "I don't like it when kids are hurt." It was as good an excuse as any for now. But I wanted her to tell me what she knew without going into my reasons for asking.

She seemed to take me in again, looking me over and sighing as though she'd made some kind of decision. "Maybe you can make progress where we can't."

I raised my brows. "You have no leads?"

"Not much, I'm afraid. I'm sure you know a zombie killed the boy, but now the family seems to be missing."

I didn't correct her on the zombie thing. I wondered if I was the only one who realized this didn't involve a zombie. Did they know Vivian was connected to this in some way?

"Was the family taken when the kid was killed?" I narrowed

my eyes. Surely if Vivian had something to do with this family going missing, she wouldn't have sent me down there to look at the crime scene.

None of this made sense, a fact that was eating at me despite the fact I should just be done with Vivian and walk away.

"We don't know." She scrubbed a hand over her face. "Hell, I shouldn't be telling you this, but the neighborhood isn't exactly trusting of cops. Most of the time, people there look to Gransen for protection. That, or they move away if trouble starts. It's entirely possible that's what happened to the Connors. It looked like someone grabbed the boy from his room. Took him out through the window. If the family saw him get killed and ran, or if they were taken— we don't know."

She was worried about getting caught sharing information with me, but what the hell did she have to share? Not a whole hell of a lot, it seemed.

"Roxie!"

I heard shouts as dragons filled the space out front of the cabin. Officer Adams was on her feet, weapon raised and pointed at the door.

I stood and put out a hand to stop her as Adak and Dash barreled through the door. I was more than a little impressed my little brother had shifted as fast as the alpha of his pack had, but I also couldn't suppress the nerves that he'd done so.

When I got him alone, I needed to remind him to tamp down the displays of his strength. We didn't need people questioning his power.

Dash grabbed me by the shoulders and I winced. Damn I was sore as hell.

"I'm good. Just a little run in with some high winds."

Adak growled behind Dash and I rolled my eyes at his glare. What the hell was he pissed off about?

Did he think I'd called the police? Maybe he didn't think

human police departments should be involved with myth matters?

"Aster, can you see if you can heal some of Roxie's wounds?" His glare didn't cease as he spoke.

Maybe that was his issue. Maybe he was ticked off that I'd be using pack resources again.

I held up my hand to stop Aster. "Thank you but there's no need, Aster. It's just a few cuts and bruises."

It was bullshit. There was a pain in one of my legs that said there was something more going on there. I'd torn something.

Aster seemed to know it and she snorted her assessment.

The alpha shot a finger at the couch. "Sit!"

Oh hell no, he didn't.

Except he did. And from the look on his face, it was more than clear he fully expected me to obey.

I wanted to say "There will never, ever be a time when I respond to your commands like a lap dog," but before I could, Dash stepped in.

"Roxie, please," Dash said, his eyes shooting from me to Adak and back again as he took hold of my arm. "Please just let her look at you."

My breath wooshed out as I rubbed my face with my hands. This was how this was going to be from now on. I had somehow ended up with the police in my living room and me taking orders from an overbearing alpha dragon.

In a matter of days, everything in my world had spiraled completely and utterly out of control.

19

Roxie

I jogged back down the long drive in front of the cabin for the fifth time glad for the healing from the pack witches. The run up the drive was a good workout and the jog down was a test in agility as my feet skittered over rocks and hopped large crevices in the rough terrain. Maybe I'd come out here one day and flatten some of the bigger drops and fissures. My sedan wasn't made for riding on land like this.

Leaves rustled to the left of me and I turned, hand on the knife at my lower back. What stepped out of the woods shocked the hell out of me and that wasn't all that easy to do.

I knew the soft gray muzzle that came out of the bushes instantly. He was as familiar to me as one of my knives: a gray pit bull with white that ran from the underside of his chin down his chest and through to his belly. He had a sleek muscled body and a chunky head with hair so short and fine it was like petting silk when I ran a hand over him.

Ghost wriggled, nearly bending his body in half in his happy dance at having found me.

I knelt, feeling nothing but awe for the little creature in front of me. It was really him.

"How in the world did you get here, baby?"

I put my arms out and let him come to me. He circled in my arms, the sensation of him rubbing that soft fur against me making my chest go tight. I hadn't expected to feel that again and I felt the telltale burning at my nose that meant the tears in my eyes might spill over if I didn't get a handle on my emotions.

"Buddy, how did you find me?" He rubbed his square head against my thigh and wriggled harder at my words. "How in the world?"

He didn't answer me. Just kept up his wriggly-wiggly dance.

I ran my hands over him, checking for I don't know what. He'd crossed hundreds of miles to find us.

The bottom of his paws looked good, but small ridges on his shoulders felt like maybe he'd been scraped up and had scabs forming under the fur.

"Did you bang yourself up getting back to us?"

Guilt stabbed at me. I should have found him. Should have waited. He might not technically belong to me, but he had become mine the first time he wiggled his little butt at me.

I smelled Adak's campfire scent seconds before he stepped into view.

"Who's this?" Adak was looking at Ghost like he might be a bomb masquerading as a pit bull.

"Ghost."

"There are no such things as ghosts."

I laughed at that. Sure, I knew there weren't really ghosts. There were remnants—wisps of energy caught in a repeating cycle that might seem like ghosts to the uneducated. And there were revenants— horrific creatures of dredged together spirits torn from the underworld by death magics practitioners. But there were no true ghosts.

This was gonna be fun. "Oh yeah? Give him a little pat and then talk to me about ghosts." I nodded at the dog who was watching Adak warily.

Adak shot me a look, then put his hand out to touch the dog.

Ghost blinked out of existence. Adak's eyes shot to mine, surprise but also keen interest in the gold that swirled there. I liked that I'd surprised the alpha. Something told me it wasn't easy to do.

"Back up a couple of steps," I said.

Adak did and Ghost blinked back into existence tucked behind my leg, looking at Adak.

"Well that's ..." Adak scrubbed a hand over the side of his face, head tilted at the dog. "Huh."

I laughed at his puzzled expression. "Ghost. That's Ghost." It had taken time for Ghost to remain corporeal to my touch but his hugs made it all worth the effort at earning his trust.

When I stood, Ghost pressed against my leg. When I took a step, he stepped with me.

"I guess you don't need a leash." Adak's tone was wry but I could see the humor flashing in his eyes.

"Who knows? Up to this minute, I thought he'd stayed behind in—" I cut myself off. No need telling Adak where we'd been last. The less people knew about us, the better.

"Why did Gransen pay you that visit last night?" Adak asked.

"Mostly to see if he could get Dash to join his crew. I told him no and he didn't like that."

Adak crossed his arms over his chest, arms bulging with the move. I couldn't help but notice his hands. Large, with the evidence of work on them. Calluses that showed he wasn't an alpha who left the hard work to his pack.

I spent a split second imagining the feel of those hands on my body but shoved that thought into a box with shackles and chains to keep it at bay. I'd scratch that itch outside my brother's pack.

"He had his goons tear down half your woods because Dash won't join his pack?"

I shrugged. "That and he's pissed about a case I'm working on."

"A case?"

I turned and headed back toward the cabin, walking now. "A child was killed in what Gransen has now explained to me is his turf."

"How many of them?"

"Huh? How many what?"

"How many dragons came after you?" he asked.

"Four. Well, five with Gransen."

He was studying me. The asshole was trying to figure out how I walked away from that fight.

I got it. When humans looked at me, they might be impressed. I'm a six-foot-tall Black woman with a lot of muscle to my frame and scars to prove I've been in my share of fights and come out alive.

Myths, though? They didn't see that. They saw a human, and in the myth world, humans were weak. Not something to respect or fear.

"Didn't your witches tell you they had to burn two bodies?"

He gave a slow nod. "They did."

I shook my head. He was trying to figure out who had killed those dragons. Surely it couldn't be little old me.

"You know he's a stone-cold killer, right?" he asked.

"Gransen?"

He nodded.

I had a question of my own. "You chased him out of your territory?"

Another nod from the alpha.

"Why not take him out if he's attacking people in your territory?"

From what I'd seen of Adak and his people, they had to be able to do it. Though maybe I just hadn't seen Gransen at his full power yet. He'd been toying with me, for sure.

Adak was more open than I thought he'd be. "Eliminating Gransen would create a power vacuum in Austin. Shifting the balance of power means lives lost. It means the council might gain a stronghold to come in and take over."

"And you don't want that? The council, I mean?"

He didn't answer. Only shrugged off the question and kept moving like we were taking a stroll, not discussing killing off his enemies and juggling international politics.

I had a feeling I knew why he wouldn't want the council here. The council was an international organization made up of myths and humans from all countries. Many people thought they were too far removed from cities and states to be involved in local government.

I happened to agree.

"What else can you tell me about him?" Might as well push Adak for what he would tell me about Gransen. It looked like I'd be dealing with Gransen whether I wanted to or not.

"He's been pushing out the edges of his territory lately, even mixed up in some stuff over the border into Mexico. I don't want him thinking he can get too close to our territory. I don't want anyone in this city getting that powerful, but especially not someone as sick as he is."

I waited for more. This must have been what Officer Adams meant when she'd said Gransen was expanding his empire.

Adak filled the silence. "You know he's a water dragon?"

I hadn't known. I hadn't seen him shift yet and I couldn't always tell what type of dragon someone was unless I saw them shift and use their powers.

Adak went on. "He likes to punish anyone who defies him or lets him down with a bucket of water trick. He stands them in front of a bucket of water, then uses his power to force the water down their nose and throat, choking them. He draws it back out and shoves it back in again and again. His little twist on waterboarding."

I grunted. Great. I'd made enemies with a sadistic doughboy on a power trip who liked making water balloons of peoples' lungs. Goodie.

20

I wasn't gentle when I rapped on Vivian's door. Okay, I didn't rap at all. Thump, thwack, bang. Those might better describe what my fist was doing.

Five minutes of banging and she wasn't coming to the door. I left the front porch and looked through the window to the left of it, Ghost on my heels, looking up at me.

It was a den with couches and chairs and a whole lot of the flowy purple scarves she liked draped over the furniture in what must be her idea of interior design.

It was also empty. I went to the window on the other side of the front door. A darkened room. As I traipsed around the outside of the house, Ghost watched my movements, puzzlement clear in the dog's expression.

I stopped and fisted my hands on my waist when we'd made it back around to the front.

"Damned hedge witch. I never should have taken a job from her in the first place."

Ghost let out a woof. He agreed.

I looked up at the second floor of the house. All the lights were out.

If it would do any good, I'd break in and destroy the bonding candle but you couldn't break a bond that way. Only the holder of the bond or the holder's death at another's hand could break it.

"Let's see if we can figure out why she hired me to kill this zombie."

I had filled Ghost in on the whole case on the drive down, so I was going to pretend he knew what I was talking about as he happily followed me to the car. He also happily napped on the seat next to me as I drove. He was good at that.

I probably should have more respect for the crime scene seal that was across the door at the Connors' house but honestly, it had been more than a week since the boy's murder. If the police hadn't done their job inside yet, they should just step aside and let someone else have a crack at it.

Picking the lock was easy. It was a quick matter of scrubbing the pick along the pins until they settled into place. With a lock this cheap, it took me seconds to get in.

I slipped in through the back door and shut it behind me, taking a minute to listen to the house. I had spent hours growing up sitting still and silent so that the smallest of sounds could reach me in the cacophony of background noise. It was a skill Mom made Dash and I practice, and it was one of the things I was glad she'd taught us. It had saved our lives more than once.

Silence greeted me in the house, but it wasn't ordinary silence. It was heavy, like the house was holding onto the horror that happened there.

I wasn't about to open curtains or turn on lights. It wasn't a part of town where people were likely to watch out for anything suspicious and call the cops, but the last thing I needed was one of Gransen's thugs realizing I was back here. I didn't want to be the special guest at one of his water bucket shows.

Ghost bumped my leg and I looked down, wondering if I could tell him to stand guard at the back door for me. With the way he'd glued himself to my leg, I didn't see that happening. He hadn't left my side since he'd shown up that morning.

More than once, I wondered how in the world he found me. He couldn't have tracked us by scent. At least, I didn't think that was possible since we'd traveled by car.

But if I needed any proof Ghost wasn't a normal pit bull, I only had to look at the way he could vanish when he got scared or startled. So my not-so-normal little pittie had some ability to magically track. It was my best guess at an explanation.

"You let me know if you hear anything, you hear?" I said to the big hazel eyes that looked up at me.

He ducked his head in a bob like he'd understood and I smiled. Two sets of ears were better than one. Not to mention, it was kind of cool having company on a job.

We moved through the house and I began to pick up scents. My nose wasn't any stronger than the average human, but I was more practiced at using it than most people and I knew myths' scents. That gave me an advantage even if I wasn't a bloodhound.

"Nymphs," I said, looking around. Based on the number of plants in the home, I was guessing they were garden nymphs. There hadn't been any garden in the backyard, but here, there were potted plants on every surface, fragrant flowers in bloom in many of them. I wondered if the nymphs were trying to hide who they were. Nymphs couldn't resist having plants of some kind in their life—hell they needed them for survival—but they weren't flaunting it to anyone outside this house.

There was another scent, too. Musky and rich. It was the earthy scent I'd picked up outside, but it was growing stronger, even as the flowers tried to douse it.

If I had to guess, I'd say it was a chimera.

With the head and shoulders of a lion, body of a goat, and snake head tail, the things were powerful. The beast was also a shifter. It could take on a human form, although in true creepy fashion, the snake tail stayed in the human form.

His scent was all over here. If he was the killer, would it be this pervasive? I didn't think so. The killer's scent would only be here on the surface. The chimera and the nymphs' scents were blended together, intertwined and overlapping.

I followed a hallway and found a master bedroom and two children's rooms. One had a bunk bed but only one level looked like anyone slept in it. The other, a single bed and a window that someone boarded up. I stepped into that one.

The bed was messy with a blanket trailing on the floor beside it and its pillow half on the nightstand and half on the bed. The smell of panic hovered in the air. I didn't want to picture the child as his attacker dragged him through the broken window, but I did. It was my job.

I stepped to the window. The intruder broke it from the outside and I found blood on the sill.

I bent and sniffed the blood. It smelled of grass and flowers. Nymph. The boy's most likely. No eau de zombie, though.

In fact, I only smelled the nymphs and the chimera in the house. And that made my stomach lurch. Could one of the parents have done this to the kid and that was why I only smelled the family here?

I recalled two boxes of cereal on the table with bowls and spoons stacked neatly next to it, like someone had prepped for breakfast but never made it to the meal.

The family had run. Maybe they hurt the kid and then took the other one and ran?

I looked down at Ghost. Could he track them? And what did I do? Hand him a shirt and say "show me where he is, Lassie?"

I tilted my head at the dog and he tilted his right back. I tilted the other way and he followed the gesture with his own.

"Goofball." Couldn't help but smile.

I went to the master bedroom, not really knowing why I wanted to keep looking, other than to know if Vivian had some reason for sending me out on this job. I wanted answers.

There was a queen-sized bed and it looked like two people slept in it. One side smelled distinctly like a garden nymph, the other the chimera. I was guessing the garden nymph was the mom going from the long strands of blond hair that decorated the pillow on the less smelly side of the bed.

I turned to leave the room and froze. Written on the wall in scorch marks were the words, "Return or I kill the other boy."

That didn't seem like something one of the parents would write. Unless this was a case of a domestic dispute going sickeningly, hauntingly wrong.

Something made my feet move back to the dead boy's room. Something that needled at the back of my mind like an ice pick to the skull.

I stood in the boy's room, letting my gaze skip over the contents of the room. No scent. No hairs or prints or anything left behind.

There was only one myth that had no scent whatsoever. I remember Mom talking about them once, but a jinn wouldn't be here. Shouldn't be here. Made of smokeless fire, jinn were brutal, deadly, and scary. Not to mention incredibly rare.

It couldn't possibly be a jinn.

Maybe it was a charm or spell, something that covered the scent of a person or myth. Not that I'd ever heard of that before, but it was easier than believing my jinn theory.

If it was a jinn, why didn't he just set the house on fire if he was after this family? Smoke them out. Why drag one boy out and slaughter him in such a brutal, public way?

If a jinn was here, coming after this family, my guess was

that someone else was controlling it. For the most part, they lived as far away from others as they could manage. They made introverts look like party animals. So what would bring one to Austin, Texas to hunt down a chimera and some nymphs?

I went to the windowsill and bent to look at it more carefully. Only the slightest of scorch marks marred the wood on one side.

"Well, hell." I looked at Ghost. He lowered his head.

I had a brief vision of a chimera and a jinn in a boxing ring with a flashing sign that said, "Battle of the Beasts."

Problem was, I didn't know who would win that one. Since the chimera had taken his family and run, I was guessing he didn't know either.

And that's when it hit me.

Mom's voice rang out in my head, crystal clear. "You'll need the goat and the young ones."

Well, damn.

21

THIS WAS PROBABLY A MONUMENTALLY bad idea. I looked out at the woods at the back of the cabin. I'd already just about destroyed the woods on one side fighting Gransen's dragons. Most of the woods at the back hadn't been touched by the magic burns yet. It would really suck if I took it out with a real fire at this point.

From what I'd heard on the radio on the drive home, I couldn't count on any help if I did start a fire. The Austin Fire Department was battling fires all over town, which confirmed my jinn theory. I was betting the jinn was hunting the Connor family and attempting to burn them out each time he got close.

Whoever had sent him wanted to make sure he sent a message. Not only to the Connor family, but to anyone else who crossed him. It was the only thing that made sense. Otherwise, the jinn would have simply grabbed the family and brought them back to whoever had told them to "return."

Or grabbed both kids and held them until the parents returned.

Returned to who, I didn't know.

Ghost circled my feet as I debated how much lighter fluid to put on the coals. Buying the small portable grill had been as much of a splurge as buying the steaks had. With the way the magic burns took out plants, it now cost a lot more to buy anything that relied on plant life, including meat and poultry.

I squirted what I thought was a decent amount of lighter fluid over the coals and looked again at the two steaks waiting on the plate, then the woods at the back of the house. Woods I very well might set on fire. Maybe it would be better to put them in the microwave and hope for the best.

"You might want to back up," I said to Ghost as I took a step back myself. I should have looked for those long matches when I was at the store. Instead, I struck one of the shorties against the side of the box they'd come in and tossed it onto the coals.

The whoosh and resulting flames were a lot bigger than I thought they'd be.

Ghost was whimpering as we both scuttled back to avoid the fireball and I ran my fingers over my eyebrows, checking for damage.

"Okay, not so much lighter fluid next time."

I looked to the plate with the steaks and hoped like hell this was going to work. "Do I pop them on the fire now or wait for this to die down some?"

The dog didn't answer, unless you counted a head tilt.

"If you're hoping for some of this steak, the least you could do is try to make sure I don't screw it up too much."

He laid down, head on paws.

I watched as the flames started to recede and the coals began to turn white at the edges. "Here goes," I muttered as I tossed the two steaks onto the flames. "Don't think you're getting a whole one for yourself," I said to Ghost.

I watched the flames flare up and surround the steaks, wondering if that was normal.

Ghost didn't give me a head tilt this time. He had wandered away from the grill and was sniffing around the grass. I watched him while I debated whether to close the lid on the steaks or not.

If I hadn't been watching him, I wouldn't have noticed the air ripple around him when he moved past a small area at the edge of the tree line.

"Well, that's interesting." I left the grill, deciding it was better to leave it open so I could see if the meat caught fire and walked to the spot Ghost had just disturbed. I hadn't come back here much which could be why I hadn't felt the fold before.

But it was there. When I got close, I could feel a magic fold the same as I felt the much larger fold Nova Force hid their pack in. Adak's fold was enormous. I could only feel this fold when I got right up to it which told me it was small, but it was there.

I braced myself and stepped into the fold. If there was a ward, I would feel the pain when it kicked me back before I was able to cross the boundary.

Here's hoping that didn't happen. I'd dealt with enough aches and pains lately. I didn't need to be adding to that.

I felt the normal shock of magic skittering along my bones, and the sludgy disorientation of crossing a magical boundary, the zip of the needles as the magic dug in and took hold, and then I was through.

It was small alright. I stepped back out and called Ghost to me, so he'd follow me through. Not that the space had much room for us.

On the other side of the fold was a small patch of grass and one tree. Not large enough for a house, but it was good to know it was here. If I needed it, I could use it to hide. And if I really saved up, I could hire a coven to stretch the fold and turn it into something large enough to build a house in someday. That way, the cabin would be nothing more than a dummy house. I could ward the entrance to the fold and live in it where I'd be a lot safer.

I stepped back out of the fold. It would be useful someday. I might be able to afford to have it stretched in a couple of years, but at least for now, it was a hidey hole.

"Damn!" I ran to the grill looking at the damage to the steaks.

"I'm pretty sure the blackened part of blackened steak comes from the seasoning you put on it, not from charring it past recognition."

Adak stood next to the grill smirking as I ran to save my dinner. The list of things I needed to get was growing. Enough money to have the fold stretched to accommodate a house, money for a ward on the fold, and an alarm that told me when someone had entered the property outside the fold since I obviously couldn't hear out here when I was in there.

That or I could invest in a bell to put around the big guy's neck if he was going to continue to come around.

Yes, I was grinning at the thought of it.

Why did he keep showing up? Was it normal for him to keep such close tabs on new people in his territory?

Heat bit at my hands as I tried to stab the burnt steaks and slide them onto a plate. "Dang." That hurt.

Adak stole the fork from me, reaching in and removing the steaks easily even as the flames nibbled on his skin. I guess it made sense that heat and flames didn't bother a fire dragon.

Said fire dragon was looking at the meat like it was a science experiment.

I sighed and snagged the plate, walking to the small table and chairs on the back porch with Ghost on my heels. Adak placed the lid over top of the grill and closed the little slat that let the smoke out.

"That looks … interesting." Adak invited himself to sit in the chair next to me, his long legs stretched out in front of him as he eyed my dinner.

I sawed into a corner of the meat.

"New to cooking?" he asked mildly, humor dancing in his eyes.

He knew damned well and good I was new to cooking. Dash had made that abundantly clear.

I worked on relieving my steak of a good-sized chunk of itself instead of reminding him my dinner usually came in a can.

The meat was already in my mouth by the time I realized I should have cut a smaller piece. It was tough, nothing more than char at the edges, the middle chewy and overdone.

At least I hadn't done a horrible job of seasoning it. I'd put a lot of salt and some black pepper on it before cooking it to within an inch of its life, so the flavor wasn't half bad.

Adak was laughing at me as I worked my jaw. I wouldn't give him the satisfaction of pushing my plate away. I forced the bite down and began cutting another.

Ghost eyed me hopefully so I tossed the next piece to him. He appreciated my cooking, but he swallowed his bite without chewing. Maybe that was the key to this. I needed to cut small enough pieces that I could swallow them whole like Ghost did.

"I came by to make sure you were alright. I heard you were back down in Gransen's territory today. Wanted to make sure he didn't give you any trouble."

"How do you know what I was doing today?"

He only offered a shrug.

I sent him a look that I hoped said I wasn't planning to talk until he did. I think my efforts to masticate the shoe leather in my mouth might have ruined the effect of my glare.

I put the plate with the rest of the steak on the floor for

Ghost. He didn't hesitate to dig in and his jaw seemed to be able to handle my cooking just fine.

I could do cold cereal for dinner.

Adak gave in. "I have people down in Gransen's territory who are faithful to me. A few shop owners. Couple of restaurants. They told me you stopped in to ask about Jake Connors."

"The convenience store or the coffee shop?"

"Both."

Huh. Just how deep did his reach go?

"Have you ever dealt with a jinn?" I asked.

Adak sat forward at that. He looked at me long and hard for a minute before speaking. "We'll get you moved onto the pack lands tonight."

I snorted. It wasn't ladylike, but hell, I couldn't stop myself. He'd gone from telling me I needed an invitation onto his lands when I wouldn't join the pack, to telling his seconds-in-command I wasn't what I seemed, to telling me he was moving me in with the pack.

"It's killing you that you can't control me, isn't it? That I'm not just begging for protection from the almighty Nova Force."

His jaw ticked. "A jinn is nothing to mess around with. I don't care how much your mother taught you when you were growing up. She didn't prepare you for that."

I slid my chair back and stood. He'd been talking to my brother. More importantly, Dash had been talking to him. Telling him shit that was my business and my business alone.

I needed to have a talk with my baby brother.

Still, Adak had no idea what growing up with my mother was really like. You could tell people stories, but unless they'd lived it, they just didn't get it. People had a way of underestimating just what kind of training I'd had.

I picked up the plate Ghost had licked clean. "I got this. I won't be moving into your guest house tonight or any other night."

The look on his face was priceless. It was a combination of confusion—I was guessing he didn't hear "no" a whole lot—and frustration. Frustration that looked to be turning to temper.

"Close your mouth, Alpha Man. I'm heading to bed. You know the way off my land."

I think I heard one of his teeth break when I turned to go into the cabin. That man's dentist was probably going to send me a bill soon.

22

My research showed the legends around jinn often revolved around myths of demons and even Satan. Some believed Satan was a jinn so feared and reviled for his fascination with cruelty and manipulation that he earned a heightened place among other jinn.

Arabic cultures often talked about jinn as heartless manipulators bent on destruction and injury.

There were African records that talked about jinn as spirits who could be either evil or benevolent, but when Mom told me the stories, she'd never mentioned any benevolent ones.

The Illieri are African and our heritage reflected that, but many of the stories we told were different than those of other African clans and peoples. The tales of my people warned of Dabria's return to earth one day. Of the Goddess Lilliera's greatness and how we would stand by her side when she returned to our realm to fight Dabria someday.

They weren't bedtime stories.

At some point, stories about jinn had been anglicized and they'd been called genies. They were romanticized as someone who would grant three wishes to anyone who freed them from a bottle.

The truth was, any wishes granted by a jinn were simply a way for the jinn to twist whatever their victim wanted into something punishing that would bring more harm than good to the one making the wish.

In recent centuries, jinn had mostly removed themselves from interacting with the mortal world. They tended to be indifferent to humans and myths nowadays which was why it was so strange to see this one coming after the chimera and the nymph.

Still, I didn't have a way to kill this thing. A few of the entries I'd found in online blogs and things talked about jinn being susceptible to magic. That should mean I could kill it.

But there were no stories of how that could happen. Which told me this was more than just taking its head or a stake through the heart.

I kept digging, going to more and more obscure sites on the internet. Hours later, I found a single mention of a spelled stone blade. I knew that meant a vessel, but I didn't know where I could get one or how to use it.

Maybe the cop I'd met, Lorna Adams, might have information. Of course, she might see my asking about a way to kill a jinn as premeditation.

Technically, I could kill a myth in self-defense or in defense of another and I probably wouldn't even have to go through a trial to prove it was self-defense. But arming myself with something that would allow me to kill or trap a jinn while I went out hunting for one didn't seem like a smart thing to talk to a cop about.

My contacts in Austin were limited. I blew out a breath and stretched my arms above my head. Right now, I knew the hedge witch, Hunt, and the pack. The hedge witch was dodging me and I knew I'd probably need to go to Hunt for help when it was time to track the jinn since I hadn't come up with a way to get Ghost to track for me yet. I looked toward the direction of the pack. I'd need to go to Nova Force for this.

I grabbed a soda and walked out the door, texting my brother as I did. I wouldn't mind seeing him anyway, and this was a good excuse.

The ache I had come to associate with a magic burn hit me and I stopped in my tracks. Most people said they felt a tingling at most with the burns. And unless you were an earth witch, you couldn't feel them coming ahead of time.

I never felt them ahead of time, and if it was passing nearby, I might see the devastation but not feel the magic as it rolled through, depending on the distance. But if I was in one when it passed through, it hurt like hell. Not a sharp pain. Not anything distinct.

This was more a dull, bone deep ache all through my body.

I put my hands to my knees and fought the swirl of nausea as I focused on breathing in and out, steadily. Ghost whined and licked my hand as I backpedaled inside to try to get out of its way.

When the burn passed some three minutes later, I looked out to see the straggling lawn that had fronted the cabin was now brown and there was a new ribbon of dead trees running through the woods on either side of me.

I was sure one day they'd find out a year or two was knocked off your life every time you were caught in a burn, but so far scientists were trying to tell us they only harmed plant life. It just didn't seem feasible to me, but what did I know?

I chugged water from the bottle I kept in my car and headed for the pack lands to find Dash was waiting for me outside the fold. His arms around me as he hugged me felt damn good. It had been more than a minute since we'd seen each other, and I missed him.

Dash let me loose and made a show of looking me over. I gave that same look right back to him.

He looked good. Happy.

Raised brows showed me he wasn't as thrilled with how I looked, but I was only a little bruised. Nothing too bad. He should be used to it by now.

He knelt to love on Ghost but his words were for me.

"Maybe now that I have a pack, you could get a nice job in …" He hesitated.

I shot him a warning glance and he grinned.

"A library? A museum? Maybe a toy store. You know. Something safe and quiet."

I shook my head at him, but I was laughing. How could I not? The image of me sitting in a library reshelving books with my scars and knives strapped to my body was more than a little entertaining.

"Speaking of jobs, what does the pack have you training to do?"

He stopped walking just before the clearing where the lair was and turned to me. I'd seen the way he was shuffling his feet and looking at the ground before he turned. That was my baby brother's go-to move when he wasn't sure how to say something.

I made a get on with it motion with my hand.

"I, um, it turns out I'm uh…" Dash glanced up toward the house. The field was empty so we were alone for now. "I'm turning out to be pretty powerful at stuff. Things like that molten breathing thing and um, I can do some flying stuff they don't expect a dragon my age to be able to do, so they have me training for the guard."

Shit. A pack's guard meant their fighters. The myths they'd use if they went into battle for any reason. The ones who would defend against any attack on the pack.

That wasn't what got to me. He would have to fight someday. That was our reality and we both knew it.

No, the problem wasn't that he would be fighting.

I shook my head and stepped closer, putting a hand on his shoulder. "You can't stand out, Dash. Not until we know we can trust them."

"I *do* trust them, Rox."

I tightened my grip on him and shook him. Not hard, but enough to wake him up. He was being foolish. "No, Dash. Not yet."

"Yeah I get it," he said, rubbing a hand over his short-cropped hair. "If they figure out what I am."

He didn't have to finish that sentence. No one could know he was egg-born. If people knew that, there would be a hell of a lot of questions about where he came from and how me and Mom ended up with him.

Dash didn't look happy, though, and I didn't blame him. What I was asking him to do was hold back on what he was capable of. Hide himself from the people he'd now made his family. Lie to them.

I put a hand on his shoulder. "Dash, I'm sorry. Just hold back a little until you're really one of them. Until we're sure they can handle knowing."

He nodded, but his eyes were on the ground now and I knew I'd hurt him. When he looked up again, he'd hidden his emotions behind a mask and I hated seeing that.

Before I could say anything else, I saw twenty or more witches come around the side of the cabin to the front door, some leaning on one another as they moved. One of the female dragons I'd met during the bonfire had two witches leaning on her, one on either side.

"The burn hit you up here, too?" I asked. I hoped they got to their crops in time to protect them. They had a lot of mouths to feed, including my brother's.

Dash glanced over his shoulder at the witches before nodding at me. "Clay warned everyone in time."

"Clay?"

Dash nodded and pointed toward the man I'd seen sitting at the campfire with Brenda the other night. He wasn't smiling in the same excited way this time, but the look on his face as he helped one of the witches walk was pure pride.

"He's an earth witch. Powerful. Growing up in another coven, he was treated really bad because he's like disabled or something, but Brenda found him and brought him here when he was a teenager. I guess she's kind of like his mom now. He feels the magic burns before they reach the crops and raises the alarm."

That was good. Real good. I liked knowing Dash's pack had the kind of resources they did to protect their food sources.

"You said you needed help with something?" He started walking across the clearing toward the lair.

I answered his question as I caught up to him. "Is there anyone here who might be able to tell me how to kill a jinn?"

Dash stumbled but caught himself. "Fuck, Rox, a jinn? Are you serious?"

"You think I'd make it up?"

"No, but damn woman, a jinn?" He shook his head, sounding more like a parent than my kid brother. "I leave you alone for a week and you're taking on a jinn."

"Don't sass me. Besides it wasn't by choice. You remember I told you Mom left a note in the cabin? She said I'd need the goat and the young ones. This jinn is hunting a chimera and his kids."

Dash's lips pursed but I could see he knew better than to tell me to ignore one of Mom's visions. You didn't do that, even if it meant taking on a jinn.

"Are you sure this means the chimera? He's only part goat."

I shook my head. "I'm not taking a chance. If we need them, we need them."

I'd ignored Mom's visions one time. We had lost Mom as a result.

Never again.

"It won't do any good if you're dead." We had stopped again in the middle of the field now and Dash was glaring at me.

I gave him the same look back. Mom had seen him saving the world, not me. If I could be by his side at the end, great. But first I had to do all I could to make sure he made it to whatever this big battle was.

"Little brother, you really gonna sit here and lecture me on this shit? This is my job. It's what I do."

He glared a minute longer, but I waited him out. I had years on him.

"You need Marat," he said when he finally broke. "He's the pack librarian and archivist. I'm pretty sure there's nothing he doesn't know."

"Take me to him?" I asked, but he had already turned to lead the way. My brother might not always like my choices, but he'd always have my back.

23

MARAT WAS A DRAGON, though I couldn't place what his affinity was. He didn't smell like a fire dragon. He had close cropped, perfectly white hair. His dark brown skin and the deep kale green color of his eyes might label him as earth, but that was really just a guess. Eye color didn't always hold any clues.

His eyes were nice, even though I hated kale. Why did kale have to be one of the things that withstood a magic burn so well? I mean, why couldn't baby soft lettuces be something that withstood a burn so they'd be cheaper like kale?

My mouth watered as I remembered the salad they'd served when I ate dinner with the pack that first time. They really had ruined me for other food.

The dragon with the green eyes gave only a slight glance to the Velcro dog at my calf before he pulled out a book that was more of a tome based on its size.

How much knowledge did the pack have stored away in the stacks of shelves that lined the room? The books all looked like they might be centuries old and likely more than that. I wondered if they had it all digitized or if Marat had an index of epic proportions in his head.

He'd gone straight to the volume he pulled down and was now flipping through the old pages like he knew right where to go.

"Jinn are nasty business for a human to go up against." He looked at Dash. "Does Adak know about this?"

I bit down on my cheek to stop from snapping that Adak wasn't my keeper. I had a feeling this man would be able to tell me exactly what I needed to know. I didn't want to do anything to keep him from helping me.

Dash shook his head. "Roxie can take care of herself. She's not your average human."

Marat eyed the arsenal of weapons I had on display with pursed lips. I held his gaze, my spine straight. I was used to this routine from people who hadn't seen me fight.

I was human, but I was the daughter of Adira, the Wrath of Lilliera. I was Illieri, with centuries of warrior blood in my ancestry. I had decades of training and a mother who made sure that training stuck.

He seemed to come to some conclusion and turned the book my way, pointing to the page he'd opened it to. I looked at a picture of a being that was roughly human in shape but taller and made of flames. It might be all heat, but its eyes were cold as ice.

"Nothing but smokeless fire so they're extremely hard to kill," Marat said. "You might think a good hose would do the trick but water doesn't affect them. Wind doesn't either. This is magical fire. You need to trap it in a vessel and then destroy the vessel."

"So 'no' on the mayonnaise jar." I had heard of a vessel before. Mom had been pretty thorough on teaching Dash and I about most things myth and magic, as well as training us to fight.

Marat's expression confirmed how weak my attempt at humor had been. "It's not a vessel in that way. This is a magical vessel, usually in the form of a dagger or very occasionally a small sword. A witch carves it of sandstone and the coven of three must imbue it with magic. Otherwise, it's just a pretty trinket."

I waved away his explanation with my hand. I knew all of that. The coven of three referred to three covens working together in the same way three covens had made Dash. It didn't happen often. For one thing, you needed the right mixture of magic in the covens. Each of the four elements had to be represented and they had to agree to work together.

More than that, any working of a coven of three required a sacrifice. If would often be the giving of a life, so it wasn't something people lined up to do.

I'd read that the life had to be voluntarily given, so at least there weren't covens out there kidnapping people for sacrificial spell making. That was left to the death magics practitioners.

I sighed. "Not something I'm going to find in a corner store."

"Afraid not," Marat confirmed.

I caught the distinct scent of campfire smoke and turned, knowing Adak had just walked into the room. The question was, would he be in one of his Roxie-is-a-danger-to-my-pack moods or a welcome-Roxie-like-family moods?

"Hey Alpha Man." I didn't try to stop the way my hips relaxed around him, one of them kicking to the side to better show off my curves. In my head, I knew he was my brother's alpha and consequently a piss poor choice for a one-night-stand, but damn, I wanted him all the same.

I saw Dash flinch at my irreverent greeting but if Adak was irritated, he was hiding it well. Maybe his dentist had talked with him about the risk of losing his dragony fangs if he wasn't careful with all that teeth grinding.

Adak moved to the book, that prowling gate that said he could go from friend to predator in a heartbeat.

No, I take that back. He was always a predator. It was part of him the same way my curls were part of who I was.

He stilled when he saw the page with the image of a jinn.

"I thought we talked about this." Adak turned to look at me full on and he didn't look happy. Those gold eyes could go all hot and ember-like when he was pissed and that's exactly what they were doing now.

I laughed. "We did. You told me I should be afraid of the big bad jinn and I told you I'm not."

Not entirely true. I was concerned, but I wasn't going to let that stop me. Still, he didn't need to know the nuances of my emotions. Those were mine and mine alone.

"So, what, you just plan on waltzing up to it with a vessel and asking it to hop right in and let you destroy it?"

I wondered if he'd known it took a vessel to kill a jinn before this or if he'd just overheard Marat. It would be interesting to know if Adak had been researching how to kill a jinn after our earlier talk. Did he care enough about Austin and the people who lived here to go after it or would he only take it on if it came near his pack?

"Something like that." I had to admit, my plan was a little loose at the moment. "Step one is getting my hands on a vessel."

He laughed. "Marat, what's the going rate for a vessel?"

Marat cleared his throat. "20,000 dollars."

I didn't say a damned thing to that. Adak had to know that was out of my price range.

Ghost whined. Maybe the dog had some concept of money or maybe he was just reading me. Either way, he seemed to get how hopeless that was.

"For family," Marat started but Adak didn't let him finish.

Those gold eyes were on me as he spoke to his librarian. "Sometimes the best thing you can do for family is tell them no." Adak shut the book. "Sorry, we can't help."

Didn't want to help, obviously. My hips gave up their flirtation with the man and I stepped forward, spine in a rod again as I went toe-to-toe with Adak.

"It killed that boy and now it's hunting the rest of the family. You're just going to let them get slaughtered?"

Adak shook his head. "Let someone else take care of it, Roxie. You're in over your head on this."

I didn't bother to answer that one. I was in over my head on a lot of the fights I got into. It never stopped me before and it wasn't going to stop me now.

Dash was looking distinctly uncomfortable next to his alpha. Would he get in trouble for bringing me in here? Would he do it the next time I needed help?

Damn, the thought that he wouldn't cut deep and I had to shut those thoughts down before they got the better of me. Dash was bound to his pack now.

I looked to Marat. "Thank you for the information."

"I'll walk you out, Rox," Dash said, still not meeting his alpha's eyes. I didn't know how he did the submissive thing. I could never manage that.

24

I PULLED out the card the cop gave me when she came to my cabin. Officer Lorna Adams.

"Let's see what the cop can tell us," I said to Ghost as I dialed my phone.

And I'm talking to my dog more than I talk to people nowadays. Fantastic.

"You got Adams."

She didn't strike me as one for small talk and really, neither was I. "It's Roxie Andrews. Can you tell me where daggers might hang out in Austin?"

Daggers usually had a spot they would gather to network or trade information or jobs. I needed to find out where I might get a vessel and a dagger hangout could be a place to start. Hell, maybe I could even get a lead on why the hell Vivian had sent me into a case filled with lies and where she'd gone.

"Sure, there's a bar on East 12th called The Bishop's Balzac. That's where you'll find 'em. But listen, Roxie, you should know, independent daggers aren't really a thing here. It's not safe to work as an unregistered here."

Adak had said something about that once, too. "Okay, what does that mean?"

Jack Dagger had started the concept of daggers-for-hire when he started taking on jobs going after rogue myths or solving myth problems for humans a few years after the Dawn Wars ended. He was a wolf shifter who lost most of his pack in the war and didn't have much to lose when the fighting ended. He was the ideal person to hire when you needed something risky done.

Daggers could join the council registry and be licensed, but plenty worked under the table like I did. I knew some cities had unions but they weren't usually mandatory. Hell, it would probably do the cities some good to regulate and license daggers, but most hadn't yet.

Did she mean that Austin had formed a union? Registering as a dagger with the Council meant you could charge more for your work, but the registration fees were exorbitant. It wasn't something I planned to do soon and adding a union fee on top of it made it even more unattainable.

"The daggers in Austin all run under Adeline Blanchet."

I went with "okay" again for my response. I was quite the literate speechifier today.

Luckily for me, Adams was in a sharing mood. "Blanchet is the queen of Austin's vampire court. Her fury is large and powerful and she's not someone to mess with. Born in France in the 1400s if rumors are accurate. She controls the east side of town and runs the daggers. All the daggers. Takes a cut of their pay."

I looked down at Ghost. I didn't do well with authority figures like that, but I'd already caught Gransen's attention. Could I afford to piss off the vampire queen?

"Tell me there's some grace period before I have to join up?"

"I have no idea, to be honest. That's between you and her. But Roxie, I wouldn't rock the boat on that. She doesn't take a big cut from what I hear and she does offer some protections to her people. If anyone kills a dagger on the job, you can bet she's going after the killer and people know that. It cuts down on a lot of the risk daggers face here."

Her attitude surprised me. "You're really okay with this? You didn't strike me as the kind of person who would be okay with what essentially amounts to a vampire mob boss."

I could hear her sigh across the line. "Honestly, there are just bigger things for me to be concerned with in Austin. You've met Gransen. He's a lot more dangerous for the people of this city than Adeline is, provided you aren't someone going after one of her daggers."

Hearing the words, "her daggers" grated on me. I wasn't anybody's anything and I didn't plan to be.

"Besides," she said, "it's beyond my pay grade to decide to take out a vamp."

That went without saying, I supposed. One didn't arrest a vampire. Sure, there were governments here and there who thought they could contain and arrest any vamp they deemed out of line.

I'd heard of all kinds of creative containment methods the humans tried during the Dawn Wars. Some tried filling them with stakes at the extremities and leaving them pinned to the jail cell wall in the half-shriveled state that produced. In all those cases, some idiot eventually got close enough for a vamp to bite them and control their minds. The bloodbath that followed when that person released them wasn't pretty.

Texas tried draining a vampire of her blood and pulling all her teeth before tossing her into a cell. As near as anyone can figure out, she revived herself by draining every rat that skittered into her cell. She never got her teeth back, but when she got her strength back, it didn't take her but a minute to overpower a guard and steal his gun. Once someone has a bullet hole in them, you don't need fangs to drink their blood.

When the Council was created after the Dawn Wars, part of the agreement allowed for the issuance of a kill order if a vamp was draining humans to the death instead of taking a sip here or there from voluntary servants.

Daggers executed those kill orders for money. The issuing government would pay some, and sometimes private citizens or companies who were being affected by the vamp's activities would pay an even higher bounty.

I still wasn't sold on signing up for team Adeline. "What does she do to people who don't join her little gang?"

Adams was quiet for a minute. "I haven't heard of her needing to enforce anything lately but there are enough horror stories about her from back in the day that I doubt she needs to make the point. Everyone joins up, Roxie. Everyone."

I had reached my car and opened the door for Ghost to jump in thinking about all the players I'd met so far in Austin.

Gransen wasn't anyone I wanted anything to do with and this vampire sounded bat shit crazy.

Which left Adak and his pack. Even though Dash was already part of them, I wanted to know all I could about the force. "Listen, what can you tell me about Nova Force?"

There was quiet for a beat before, "Adak is a good man, a good leader. He's fair. And there's some power there. Adak's parents were part of the group that pushed for the organization of the Council, though they died before it came to fruition. Lesande—the leader of Nova Force's witches—comes from a long line of very strong witches and she's rumored to be one of their most powerful to date. Tag has some political connections, I think. His stepmother is Cass Gentry, though I'm not sure how close they are."

I wasn't sure that was a good thing. Cass Gentry definitely had power behind her as one of the myths on the Council, but her public persona said she was ruthless. I couldn't picture her as someone who would have put Band-Aids on Tag's boo boos when he was young.

"Okay. Thanks for the info Lorna."

"You bet."

I looked at Ghost in the passenger seat. "Looks like we're going to need to negotiate with a six-hundred-year-old vamp."

25

ROXIE

It wasn't hard to find the bar Lorna recommended. The Bishop's Balzac was a few blocks east from Interstate 35 on East 12th street. Motorcycles, bicycles, and cars that ranged from old junkers to sports cars lined the street out front. The dagger population of Austin was apparently a widely varied bunch.

Of note was the fact that apparently at least one other person agreed with me that the name was shite. For one thing, it made zero sense. For another, it was inviting taunting. Balzac had been painted over and handwritten letters proclaimed the place The Bishop's Ball Sac. I mean, really, how had this bishop not seen that one coming?

I found a spot at the end of the block and turned to Ghost. "Can you do that thing where you go ghost but I can still feel you're there?" I couldn't say I was surprised when he winked out of sight. I was getting the feeling more and more lately that the little pit bull could understand everything I said to him.

I pulled open the heavy wood door to the bar and entered

the darkened space. It was the kind of place with regulars and nothing but regulars. I wasn't a regular.

It was no surprise when I got a lot of looks. I glared at those closest to me and several looked away. Of course, just as many continued to openly ogle me as I walked to the bar and picked a bar stool at the end. For them, I let my hips sway and slid slowly onto the stool, knowing my ass would give them a show. You never know when you might need to turn up the charm and ask for information.

In my experience information flowed more freely with alcohol and the hint that sex might be on the table at some point.

I would have preferred to sit in a corner booth deep inside the room instead of having my back to the door the way it was, but I couldn't do that if I wanted to find anything out that could help me.

The bartender was a tall Black man with a scar running the length of his face from temple to chin. His hair was in short braids that stood up from the top of his head with the sides shaved short.

His eyes roved over the hardware in my arm and hip sheaths, but he didn't comment on it. "What're you having?"

I knew damned well any drink with alcohol would be pricey but if I ordered soda I wouldn't earn any points. "Gin and tonic."

He kept his eyes on me as he grabbed a glass and ice and began the pour. "You're new."

I got the feeling there were people around me listening for my answer. "I am."

He cracked a smile at that as he slid the glass my way and I realized what he was. He was a faun. Small points stuck out at the top of his braids, the tips of his horns only slightly visible. IIe had strong arms and a chiseled chest covered by a tight t-shirt but the bottom half of him wasn't clothed at all.

Why bother when your furry legs and horned feet provided coverage naturally?

A woman next to me with dark red hair and more than her fair share of tattoos joined the conversation. She was five feet tall at best and the hair in her ears told me she was at least part troll or gnome.

"I don't believe we've had any new daggers register with Adeline." Her cultured voice and tone didn't go with her full sleeve tattoo looks.

I would expect the woman next to me to look like a buttoned-up secretary in a business suit if I'd heard her without seeing her.

"Perhaps I missed a memo?" Her tone told me she knew perfectly well she didn't miss any memo.

I accepted the drink the bartender handed me and gave him a ten and a twenty, telling him to keep the three dollars change. I couldn't afford to drink here often. Alcohol prices tied directly to the availability of crops and the magic burns made them just as pricey as beef or vegetables.

I turned her way and crossed my legs as I sipped. "I just got into town, but someone mentioned Adeline Blanchet to me just this afternoon."

I purposefully didn't say whether I'd be signing up with the vampire or not. I was hoping to put off that conversation.

"Perfect. You can go for your interview right after your drink." She nodded at the drink like I should down it and be on my way to see this Adeline woman.

"Interview?"

It was the bartender who answered this time. "Formality, really. You look like you know what you're doing. You pledge your loyalty to Adeline, discuss the terms of your work for her, and you're good to go."

They all seemed completely sure I'd be going the Adeline fan club route.

I felt something down at my feet and looked down to see Ghost had appeared and pressed himself between the bar and my barstool. He blinked out of sight again when I looked at him.

The red head turned to talk to someone on the other side of me and I took the chance to tune into some of the other conversations in the room as I looked around. I didn't at all get the sense that she was losing track of the fact I was there.

If I made a move toward the door, she'd be right there to make sure I made it to my interview with her boss. And no doubt, any one of the people in the room would be there to back her up.

Not that she needed it if she had troll or gnome blood in her. That kind of strength meant she'd be a hard match in a fair fight.

I grinned at my own joke because, really, when did I fight fair? I could take her, and half the place along for the ride. Instead, I turned my back to her and got back to work.

I used the tiny stirring straw to slow down my drinking and swiveled my bar stool toward the room. I wasn't the only human but there weren't a ton of us by any means. Most of the humans I spied were carrying guns.

There were two wolf shifters behind me who were debating the merits of guns versus knives. I didn't get involved but I could tell them about the time I had a gun in my hand when a magic wave hit. People say magic waves don't hit technology and I mostly agree, but I felt something that day. A ripple that told me deep in my gut that if I'd been firing that weapon at the time, things could have gone truly bad.

Accounts by people online said they'd seen guns backfire during magic waves. It wasn't something that anyone accepted as truth yet, but I was sold. At least enough to be cautious about my choice of weapons.

There were three women who I would guess were witches

at another table nearby. Witches could be hard to peg in their human form. Of course, once they shifted, you couldn't miss the glow.

"I'm telling you, vamps couldn't make pizza that good. There's too much garlic in it. Besides, Adeline would make sure the daggers got a discount if it was vamps behind it."

One of the witches stage whispered. "Magic. You don't get sauce like that without magic."

Okay, mental note to find out what pizza place they were talking about. If I started to earn a paycheck, I was getting me some of this magic pizza.

At the back of the room a group of what appeared to be full-blooded trolls squished into an oversized booth as best they could. It didn't look comfortable but the group was piss drunk and beyond caring.

When a person had troll or gnome blood in them, the result was a very powerful, thick boned person with heavy brows and hair growing from the ears unless they kept it well-trimmed.

Full blooded trolls like these were usually only four or five feet tall but they were as wide as that most of the time, too. The warts and ear hair that came to their shoulders were also sure signs of their lineage.

It was the table to my left that caught my attention. There were three men—two looked human and the other might have been a witch—they huddled together and tried to keep their voices low but I could hear them. I didn't look their way but I tuned out all the noise around me and focused only on their words. Because I was sure one of them was talking about a vessel.

"I'm not shitting you. The hedge witch has one. I tried to trade her for it once but she wouldn't budge. Said it wasn't hers to sell. Well, we need it now and I say we just take it."

"How do you know she still has it? Besides, that bitch is batshit crazy. All the jobs we might get for killing this thing won't be worth it if we're walking around with a curse on us. I heard she once cursed a guy so a little piece of his dick would shrivel and fall off every time he thought of sex. Didn't take but ten damned minutes for his dick to be gone and then she started on his balls!"

If they were talking about the same hedge witch I knew, it sounded like I had my answer on where to get a vessel. And after she lied to me about this case, I had no qualms taking the damned thing from her, either.

As much as I hated to do it, I left the rest of my drink. I didn't want to be foggy headed at all when I met Adeline and since I rarely drank, I could end up drunk faster than I liked to admit.

I stood and glanced around looking for the red headed woman. She was by my side before I could take a step.

"You're ready for your interview."

It wasn't a question.

"Looks like it."

I was surprised when she led me out the back of the bar and across an alley into another building. It was an old building that looked like it should have been on the streets of New York City instead of the east side of Austin.

The burnished black door opened without a key we entered a front entrance hall with a small kitchenette on the left and what looked like a living area on the right. A large staircase lay ahead of us.

"This is where our daggers hang out in between jobs. You can come here whenever you need work or if you discover you need a partner for a particular job." The redheaded woman was waving her arm around like she was showing me the prizes on a game show, and I had to admit, the place was really nice.

As was the idea that I could simply swing into the office for an assignment instead of having to drum up work on my own.

Not cede-control-to-a-vampire nice, but nice.

There were doors down the hallway with things like "Accounting," "Records," and Secretarial Pool," the latter of which really caught my eye. Were the secretaries for the daggers to use? What the hell would they need them for?

Shit, maybe they had to write up reports and shit. No thanks.

I turned to look in the kitchen and saw one of those pod coffeemakers. We didn't get close enough for me to see if any of the pods held actual coffee.

My bet would be that most, if not all, were blends with a tiny bit of coffee and the rest some combo of rye and sumpweed. Rye and sumpweed held up better against the magical waves than coffee did and when mixed together they could remind a body of coffee.

All around us were daggers. Shifters, witches, a few humans —the humans and some myths carrying various weapons and the others oozing the kind of power that said they didn't need a weapon to get the job done.

No one seemed to mind if anyone sat on the couches and chairs with blood stains on their pants and things looked remarkably clean for all that. They must have a staff of witches cleaning the place. Or maybe pixies.

If you could find a horde of pixies, you could sometimes convince them to trade cleaning services for space in your attic. Pixies not only didn't mind cleaning, they liked it. And they were happy to take up residence in all the nooks and crannies between the studs in an attic.

There also weren't so many pixies around that you could walk out on the corner and ask one to trade with you. It wasn't that there weren't a lot of them in the world. It was more that they usually stayed hidden, never quite trusting the world enough to strike up a conversation with just anyone. You had to win their confidence, but I suppose if you had six hundred years to work your way up to it, you could make it happen.

The redhead was walking up the stairs, but she stopped, looking over her shoulder at me with the kind of expression that said I should have been two steps behind her, at most.

I put my hand out toward where I felt like Ghost was, hoping he'd correctly interpret the signal to wait down here for me. I didn't want to risk walking him into a confrontation where he could get hurt.

Then I jogged to catch up with the tattooed woman. "What's your name?"

Not that I cared what her name was but thinking of her as the red-headed troll hybrid was a little much.

"Dauphine."

She didn't offer more or ask my name. Just turned and continued up the stairs. She skipped the second story and continued right up to the third, not telling me what was behind all the closed doors we'd just passed.

When we hit the top floor, I smelled the zombies before I saw them and my hand went automatically to my knives. I counted four of them, two to a side chained on either side of the top of the wide staircase, snarling and pulling at their bindings.

Spelled silver chains are the only thing that can hold a zombie, otherwise, the brainless fuckers would break their necks trying to get to any live meat that walked anywhere remotely close to them.

Still, it took guts to walk through the narrow passage the four zombies left. Guts and a hard stomach. The stench was horrifying. Rotting meat left out in the sun as maggots fed on it, kind of horrifying.

Dauphine walked through without looking back to see if I followed.

I did.

The third floor was different than all the other floors. It was one wide open space decorated with rugs, tables, and couches that might have once graced a Parisian parlor. The comparison ended there. Here, the windows closed off, covered by floor to ceiling paintings in biblical themes.

There were no humans, shifters, or trolls up here. Other than myself and Dauphine, that was.

Nope. The third floor was for the vamps. Three draped the couches, dressed to the nines in gowns slit up high enough on the thigh that I could probably catch a glimpse of panties if I watched for more than a minute.

I didn't.

I wondered how many vamps were in Adeline's fury. There wasn't any standard number for a fury. Could be three or four, could be hundreds.

Two blondes that looked to be twins curled up on a window seat, one with a book, the other a laptop. They didn't bother to look up when we entered the room.

I could tell they were old. You could tell a vamp wasn't fresh and young by their breathing. The body would go through the motions when a vampire was first turned, still breathing even though their bodies didn't need to circulate oxygen anymore. This could go on for a few years or more, but by the time a vamp was five or so, most stopped. Looking at the breathing was like reading rings on a tree.

These vamps didn't breathe at all.

The most disturbing sight was the man stretched out in a chair with two vampires making—ahem—use of him. He was a vampire for the time being, but this guy was so fresh, he showed almost no signs of being a vamp. It was only the slight translucency to his skin and the fact I'd caught a glimpse of fang that told me he was a vamp.

I would peg him at a day or two old. He had that new vamp smell. Plus, he looked like he planned to screw his way through as many women as he could before his brain melted and he was nothing more than a slavering brainless walking chunk of dead meat. Or before they dusted him for Vamp Dust.

Those were the two options for a male vampire. Being kept as a zombie or being staked before you went zombie to be snorted as a drug.

Who knew if he'd gotten here voluntarily or not, though I'd never understood why some men would let this happen willingly? Was it the challenge? They thought somehow they'd beat the odds?

Or maybe he'd had some terminal illness and was going to die anyway. Men sometimes let themselves be turned for a big chunk of money paid to their family if they were terminally ill.

Either way, if Adeline was turning men, she was either training up a zombie army, selling zombies for someone else's army, or dealing Vamp Dust.

26

"YOU WERE RIGHT, Dauphine. She's going to be a top earner, isn't she?"

I turned to the voice and knew I was looking at Adeline. She was tall and slender. Willowy. Long blonde hair fell down her back. With her translucent pale skin and light green eyes, she looked almost ghost-like. If ghosts existed, that is.

She also looked old. A well-preserved old, but old nonetheless. Vampires aged, although at a glacial pace. She looked to be about fifty-five or sixty in human years, with gray streaked through her blond hair at the temples and wrinkling at her eyes and mouth. Pretty good for someone who had seen so many centuries.

And she didn't move like she was sixty. She stood tall and moved with ease and grace. There was no arthritis in them bones.

The feel of her power was enough to make me wonder what it would take to cut her down if a kill order came out on her.

I smiled as I thought of the ways I might stake her. She would be a challenge and then some.

Before I could object to her talking about me as if I were a prized horse to add to a racing stable, she moved. I didn't see the movement, so much as she was suddenly in front of me.

Yes, it would be a challenge.

I liked those.

She smiled, exposing gleaming white fangs, and raised a hand as though she might touch my face, then didn't. "Lovely. So powerful." She looked at the stakes on my arms and the knives at my hips. "Assuming you know how to use those."

I raised my brows.

It almost seemed like stinging bees as her power flowed over my skin. I grit my teeth and stood my ground.

"The crosses are a nice touch." I couldn't ignore them, so I figured they were a great little ice breaker.

They hung on one wall as blatant confirmation of the fact that God and Jesus didn't scare vampires in the least. Some were gold, others wood, most laden with gemstones that looked like they could pay for my groceries for ... well, for life, even if I kept up my new steak habit.

Adeline turned her attention to the walls. "They entertain me."

The small smile on her face made me think she could say the same about everything in the room. The vampires, the furniture, me. Like the way a cat enjoys toying with a mouse.

"So, you've come to swear allegiance to me as one of my daggers."

"Not exactly."

Silence shot through the air at my words.

"I see. Did you need to discuss the terms?" She put syrup in those words and the tone said I'd be an idiot to think I could discuss terms.

No way she negotiated benefits or her cut of a dagger's take.

Then again, I'd seen some of what she provided her daggers and I had to admit, it didn't seem like an entirely bad idea to work for her.

At least, it wouldn't if she wasn't a bloodsucker. The thing about vampires was that you could never trust them. They were manipulative, lying abominations of nature that would always stab you in the back if given half the chance.

Not to mention, committing myself to work for her meant giving up control and I had issues with that. Big issues.

"Not sure I'll be working as a dagger in Austin."

Most vampires could tell if you were lying. They could hear changes in your blood pressure and sometimes even smell a change in your scent.

But Mom had prepared me well. She'd taught me to lie with the same dead surety as when I was telling the truth. The key was in simply not minding the lie. If you didn't mind that you were lying to the person, if it didn't matter to you, there was no effect on your body.

I knew I'd perfected it when I was fifteen and lied to my mother's face without consequences. If I could lie to my mother, I could lie to anyone. It wasn't something Dash had mastered but I'd taken it as a challenge, and I didn't often fail when I set those for myself.

The vampire's response was a single word. "Explain."

I didn't know how that needed more explanation, but I'd give it a go. "I'm not sure I'm going to keep working as a dagger-for-hire." Okay, so that didn't tell her anything I hadn't already said. Apparently, I sucked at explanations. Or maybe I just wasn't motivated to share with her.

"Leave us." She barely uttered the command, low and soft, but all the vamps in the room stood and left, even the guy—who had to hold up his pants with one hand as one of the women led him away.

It was just me, Adeline, and the chained zombies.

She stepped closer.

I held my ground.

"It's my understanding," she said, with so much damned honey in her mouth, I knew it had to be a trap, "that you're currently working a case. In fact, I've received a complaint about you stirring up trouble in Gransen's territory. Imagine my surprise when he wanted me to get control of my dagger only to discover you were not yet mine?"

"That's not a job," I said, making sure I didn't break eye contact.

Most books would tell you not to make eye contact with a vampire. That they would mesmerize you and you'd be spreading yourself out as their volunteer blood buffet before you knew what hit you. It wasn't true. Their ability to convince people to do what they wanted came from a bite.

If she wanted to control me, she'd need to bite me. The myth came from people who were standing there one minute, then a vampire drank from them and mesmerized them into thinking the whole thing had happened in another order. Or that nothing had happened at all, until the person saw the fang holes later.

Hence, the watching her eyes. I wanted to know what she was thinking and have a half-second to defend myself if she decided to bite. She was close enough now that I'd be hard pressed to do anything about it if she did decide to bite me, but I would sure as hell go down fighting.

"It's not a job," I repeated. "A kid died. I'm going after the thing that did it to him pro bono."

She raised a delicate brow. "How noble of you."

"Thanks," I said. She didn't look like she was expecting that, but I wasn't going to share anything else with her. Not what I knew about the kid's death, not the info about the chimera and the nymphs, or my mom's premonitions.

She raised a single finger and ran the perfectly shaped nail down the side of my face. I got the feeling she was doing it just to prove she could. To remind me who was the prey and who the predator in the room.

She was underestimating me. I loved it when people did that.

She showed me her fangs. "I wish you luck, then, with this not-job of yours."

Yeah, that's what that felt like. A gesture of good will.

I stayed still until she moved away. She did the smoky moving thing and was instantly in one of the chairs at the back of the room. She lifted a glass and took a sip of what looked like red wine. It wasn't thick enough to be blood but I doubted it was only wine. She'd probably dribbled a bit of the old o-neg in her vino for seasoning.

"Of course, you'll come back and see me should circumstances change."

It wasn't a question and I had the feeling she was manipulating me in some way.

I didn't commit either way before I left the room. I still hadn't promised to work for her, but sure, I could come back. At least I had time now to figure out how to get around working for her.

As I walked through the gauntlet of zombies, I could feel the buzzing itch of her power sweeping over me. I didn't know if she was just trying to make a point or what. But whatever it was, I didn't like it.

At least the trip had gotten me a lead on a vessel. Now it was time to see if the hedge witch really did have a vessel. And figure out how I could get my hands on it.

27

Adak

I'D MADE up my mind already. "We need to take out the jinn."

Neither Tag nor Lesande argued with me. They'd both heard the same reports I had. We hadn't been able to figure out why it was here or what it was after, but it was leaving a trail of devastation across the city. Across our territory.

Lesande blew out a breath. "We'll need a vessel. I can check with some of the Oklahoma covens. One of them might have one."

We didn't often trade with any of the smaller covens in our immediate area and some of the larger Texas ones wanted nothing to do with us after we joined our packs to the coven, but there were a few larger covens in Oklahoma we'd done business with over the past. Though, usually that was a trade for supplies or a magical working they specialized in that our coven didn't, and vice versa.

A vessel was a whole other thing. It was going to cost us.

"Can we take it out without one?" I asked standing to pace

in front of the fireplace. I hated even trading for a vessel from another coven, knowing it took a life sacrifice to make one. That wasn't the kind of magic Nova Force dealt in.

I hated that Roxie was going after this thing on her own. That woman had no sense. She was going to get herself killed and leave a hole in her brother's heart even Nova Force might not be able to fill.

I growled at the thought.

Lesande shook her head at me, answering my question. "It's suicide to go after it without a vessel. There's no point. It can't be killed or imprisoned without one."

Tag spoke up. "We can slow it down, though. It's burning through North Austin. People who haven't lost their land to the magic burns are going to lose it to this creature if we don't do something."

I had to agree with him. Having a territory meant more than just ruling over that turf and calling it your own. It meant taking care of the people who lived there even if they weren't pack. It meant leading.

So far, no one other than the Connors kid had been killed, but one death—especially that of a child—was enough. And people were losing their homes, their land. With the Dawn Wars and the burns, we'd seen enough of that to last a lifetime. No more.

I'd buy a vessel if we could find one that had already been made.

"Lesande, contact the Oklahoma covens and see what they want. If they don't have one or won't make a deal, try Louisiana." I thought about who else might have what we needed. "Try Arkansas if you have to."

The covens in Arkansas didn't blink at life sacrifice. We'd never traded with them before, but I didn't want another family to lose a child if I could help it.

I turned to Tag, who waited with his arms crossed and his face somber. He knew what we'd be leading our people into.

"Put together nine teams. Send four out to patrol and have the others on standby ready to strike when the patrol teams get us a location. This ends now."

28

ROXIE

YESTERDAY, I'd wanted to find Vivian to have it out with her. Now, I might just puke and all I could think was how much easier this would have been if she'd been out again.

I wasn't uptight about sex in the least, but still. I didn't want to see Vivian straddling a man and wiggling her hips like she thought she could ride him from here to Dallas like a horse.

The men she was with had been in the bar. They hadn't been the group talking about the vessel. These three men had been at a nearby table and must have overheard the same thing I had.

I would lay money on the fact they were wolf shifters even though I wasn't close enough to feel their magic. There was something about wolf shifters that I could spot most of the time. Some of them were hairy in their human forms, though that wasn't always the case. Tag, for example, wasn't at all hairy. Bristly, maybe. But not hairy.

Most of the time, it was a combination of the hair, a spicy

scent innate to all wolf shifters, and the way they moved like they were always the hunters and never the prey.

Vivian wasn't an attractive woman and when she drank, she was a sloppy drunk. She laughed now, loud and throaty, reaching a hand to one of the other men. He took her hand and let her pull him to her and all I could think about was the way her clothes had been so dirty and her nails filthy and grungy when I met her. How were they ignoring that?

I almost had to respect the men for their iron control over the contents of their stomachs as they touched her.

I'd come up on the back edge of her property moving slowly so I could spot any wards before they triggered an alarm. In theory, Ghost was waiting for me back there, but who knew if he'd stay. I really needed to get a rope or something to tie that dog up when I needed him to keep out of a dangerous situation.

Not that he was really mine to tie up. He could come and go as he pleased, but I didn't want him following me into something that might get him hurt. I wasn't exactly known for my safe decisions and clean living.

Slipping in the back door of Vivian's house had been easy. Enough so that I worried I'd missed something, that maybe I was walking into a trap.

The three men had already been with her in the living room and from the look of things, she'd been drinking for a while.

Looked like that was their plan. To get her wasted and then search for her stash of magical items when she passed out.

Why didn't she realize they weren't getting drunk with her? She had to know drinking alcohol wouldn't do much to them since they were myths. Unless they'd somehow convinced her they were drinking wolf's bane brew or something and she was too drunk to question it.

Not my problem and I didn't want to stick around to see the

show. They could keep her busy for me while I found the vessel she supposedly had hidden somewhere.

I circled the kitchen, feeling for any pockets of magic or spells that might be hiding something.

I half listened to the sounds from the living room so I wouldn't miss it if the party stopped. Which was gross since that meant I heard it loud and clear when Vivian started begging the men to "do me hard." I wondered if it was just going to be one of them taking it for the team or if she had plans for all of them.

There was nothing in the kitchen. I looked out across the hallway again to see the four of them in various stages of undress. One of the men had taken his shirt off and was kneeling at Vivian's feet.

Yuck, yuck, yuck. Keep moving, Roxie.

I hugged the wall as I ducked from the kitchen and down the hallway to the stairs. Homes in this part of the country didn't have basements so I didn't bother to look for one.

The top floor of the house had a short hallway and two doors on either side. I went to each door to see if I could feel anything pulling me. Or anything pushing me away from any of them. That would probably be the more likely hint that she had something in there worth hiding.

I didn't get anything so I opened one and walked the edge of the room. It was a mess. I did a quick circuit of the edge of the room and then checked the closet.

Something furry skittered into the mess, but other than that, the closet looked like it was mostly more of what was in the room. Just heaps of clutter.

I left that room, hearing moans and graphic instructions Vivian was calling out. I'd need a shower when this was over.

The next room was a little neater and looked like it was Vivian's bedroom. A queen-sized bed sat at the center of the room with clothes tossed on it. A pile of shoes sat by the bed and a tall free-standing mirror took up one corner. I spent a little extra time around the mirror. Mirrors could make powerful anchors for a spell or ward, but I didn't feel anything there.

I went into a walk-in closet but didn't see much other than the loud flowy dresses and skirts Vivian seemed to like. These looked clean so either her soiled appearance was some twisted illusion or she liked to wear things a few months to save on laundering.

A connecting room turned out to be Vivian's spell room. I probably should have checked this area first. I looked over the circular table in the corner covered with a deep purple table-cloth that fell to the floor. Another free-standing mirror stood next to it.

I checked out the shelves and cabinets before turning back to the table and mirror. I moved to them and felt the remnants of magic but it didn't feel like a protection spell.

I wondered again how old Vivian was. She didn't strike me as ancient but I felt a certain power seeping from her. Hedge witches weren't born with magic. They were largely self-taught humans who had learned to siphon and use the magic remnants true myths left in their paths as they moved through life.

Hedge witches started as sort-of cookbook witches. They didn't have the ability to shift forms as a born witch could and they were nowhere near as powerful as someone born to the craft, but they could perform enough spells to prolong their life.

They achieved hedge witch status when they'd performed enough longevity spells to attain some measure of immortality. Not that it was true endless life. You could kill them. It just wasn't as easy as killing a human and they aged very slowly.

Of course, should someone find the anchor for their longevity spells and destroy it, they'd fast forward to their true age in a heartbeat, which killed 'em deader than a cockroach. I'd never seen it happen but I was guessing it was ugly.

I turned and scanned the room again, ignoring the back corner and going to the wall that faced the front of the house. The space to either side of the windows had shelves, but the books and papers scattered there seemed mundane. Phone bills, electric bills, a few recipe cards that held actual recipes not magical spells.

The books included everything from a guide to Austin to a book on bread making for beginners.

I ran my hands in the air around the shelves and when I found nothing, touched the dusty surfaces to feel for any hidden spaces or buttons. Who knew? Maybe Vivian had a hidden door or something.

It was then that I realized something was off. Every time I looked around the room, my eyes skimmed over the far corner. The feeling was so gentle, the suggestion to look away from that area so easy to accept, that it wasn't something you'd spot right away.

When I forced myself to walk toward the corner I felt my stomach go sick as I got closer. It was a spell meant to send a person crawling home to their bed and away from the area the caster wanted to protect.

I didn't turn around. I didn't head home to my bed. Two steps and I was in the corner.

She had a bureau there with a rounded front and triangle back so that it fit snug in the space. The wood was dark and felt old. The symbols carved into its front and top looked like they'd been there collecting grunge in their crevices for decades or more.

I opened the top drawer, scanning the items.

Where Vivian was sloppy everywhere else, she was neat when it came to her supplies. The top drawer held what I was guessing was her grimoire. The leather-bound book looked old and scarred and I could sense the protective spells coming off it with a vengeance. Touching it would leave a mark and it wouldn't be a light one.

Next to it were basics I'd expect in any true witch's supply closet, but hedge witches used a lot of the same tools.

I looked over my shoulder as I shut the top drawer. The sickness was receding some now and so far Vivian hadn't appeared. I didn't hear her as loudly anymore, but there were voices beneath me in the hallway. Damn, I had no time for this.

The middle drawer held stones and gems nestled in velvet. There were also herbs and dried flowers. Behind those were what looked like finger bones and teeth. Some looked human and others had to belong to wolf shifters or maybe some kind of big cat or feline shifter. I was sure the largest of the teeth was a dragon tooth.

I hadn't liked Vivian before and I sure as hell didn't like her any better now. In fact, part of me wished I'd just gone with a full-frontal attack on her home instead of doing the cat burglar thing.

If she had this type of thing, I was willing to bet she'd used the life essence of others in some of the longevity spells she was using to keep herself alive.

The bottom and final drawer held nothing useful, either. There were several lengths of birch and other woods that a witch or hedge witch would use for focusing energies during a spell as well as a few more jars of powders and something that looked a lot like tar, but no vessel.

I looked over my shoulder. The room and hallway were still empty. I heard the low tones of Vivian's grating voice downstairs. She sounded like she was singing, but her slurring told me she wasn't going to be singing long. She'd be out soon. Then I'd be dealing with my competition.

I shut the drawer and frowned at the dresser. What the hell was I going to do now? I couldn't fight a jinn without a weapon capable of capturing it or killing it. I didn't have anything that would let me go up against it. Even if I could count on my bo staff showing up when I needed it —which I couldn't—I didn't have any reason to believe that could harm a jinn.

Hell, for all I knew, one blow to the jinn's body with the bo staff and my mysterious weapon would burn to ash and be gone.

Okay, not something I wanted to think about. As much as I didn't have any control over my bo, I somehow thought of it as being mine and I didn't want to do something that meant losing it.

I ran my hands under the bottom edge of the bureau into the slight cavity between it and the floor beneath it. A divot in the wood gave way to my fingers and the bottom piece of the bureau slid out.

There were other things in the drawer, but I didn't focus on anything but the stone dagger laying in the center. It had to be the vessel.

The vessel wasn't much bigger than my hand, its surface cool and smooth to the touch. I slid it into the inside pocket of my leather jacket and zipped it up.

"Time to go," I whispered before realizing it had gone entirely too quiet in the house.

29

ROXIE

DAMN.

I turned and wasn't all that surprised to find the three daggers behind me. Apparently they were through entertaining Vivian and had moved onto the burglary portion of their evening. Just dandy.

A slick smile crossed the face of the wolf in the middle. "Look boys, this little girl did our work for us while we were busy."

Okay, first, I wasn't little. Not by a long shot. At six feet, I was usually the tallest woman in the room. My frame had never been petite and dainty. I had muscles and curves. I had substance.

Second, no way was I handing over the vessel to these guys. Who knew if they had the ability to take down the jinn even with the right tool? At least I knew I could do the job once I had the right tool.

"I could always use a little backup, boys. You did a great job with Vivian. Maybe you can seduce the jinn, and while he's taking turns making you his bitches, I can take him out."

The guy to the right was the next to open his mouth, though you couldn't really see his mouth. He had the kind of giant beard and mustache that always made me wonder if there were food scraps lost in there for all eternity. Or maybe a small family of squirrels living in its depths.

"You're the girl from the bar. New dagger in town, huh? We don't poach each other's jobs here in Austin. We respect the code."

Ah, yes the great dagger code. It was basically whatever anyone wanted it to be when it was handy.

"Perfect. My job. My vessel." It was as good a rule as any. I took a step forward. "I'll be seeing you boys."

They looked at me like I was a child they were going to have to put in time out.

Keep underestimating me, boys. You'll win this fight for me.

"Give me the vessel," one of them said. He walked toward me with his hand extended as if I was just going to place the vessel there and be on my merry way.

Sure, that would happen.

I didn't want to kill these guys. They were daggers, which in a way made them my brothers-in-arms.

And since I'd seen them in the bar, I had to assume Adeline had them under her protection. Killing them was sure to bring her down on me and that just didn't seem smart right now. I had plenty on my plate without adding an angry vamp to the mix.

Didn't mean I wouldn't give them a little beating and take off with the vessel while they were down.

I gave a quick kick to the first guy's groin. When he moved to block the blow, I threw my elbow at the side of his jaw as he came forward and knocked him out cold.

"No means no." I scolded his unconscious body like he'd just gotten handsy with me at a bar. Then I looked up to see the other two staring at me, mouths open.

So much for the element of surprise. They were still between me and the door, and I didn't see me getting out a window faster than they could get to me, so I was going to have to fight them both.

They were on me fast.

The thing is, a coordinated attack is hard to pull off without pre-planning and these guys hadn't planned. One of them fell back a little as the other took the lead.

A quick slip of my head to the side and the punch the more aggressive guy threw at me missed completely.

Reaching out, I grabbed his shirt at the collar and fell to the floor. I stuck my foot in his pelvis bone and thrust up toward the ceiling, propelling him over me. He flew, upside down, smacking his back against the wall.

But now I was lying down and the last guy was on top of me. He was fast and was almost straddling me before I could move, but I got a knee up and wrapped that leg around his back. He had my other leg pinned but at least I had some leverage now. Sitting up fast, I wrapped my arm around his neck and began to choke.

He rained punches to my ribs, which almost made me let go, but I only had to take a few seconds of damage before he would panic from lack of air. I leaned back, arching my hips up to put more pressure on his neck.

After what felt like forever, but was probably only ten seconds, his body went limp.

Good grief he was heavy. I had to push and wriggle to get out from under him and he ended up rolling, his head smacking the wall with a thud.

"I hope that leaves a mark," I said to his passed-out body.

I felt for the small stone dagger in my pocket. Still there.

No noise from downstairs so I guessed Vivian hadn't woken.

How she slept through the war above her was beyond me but thank the goddesses for small miracles. I guess these guys wore her out.

A thought hit me and I groaned. I couldn't leave these guys here. I wanted to play nice with Adeline, at least for a while, and leaving her guys for Vivian to find in her spell room wasn't the way to make friends.

Shit. This is why I didn't have friends. They're a royal pain in the ass.

I decided to go out the window and take them with me.

One by one, I dragged them to the window and hauled their sorry asses up and over the sill. I tried to lower them easily, making the fall as short as possible, but I was sure they'd still hold a grudge about the extra bumps and bruises when they woke up. Hopefully they would appreciate the fact that I hadn't left them for Vivian to annihilate.

The one I had thrown against the wall woke up as I was making my final heave over the edge of the window. He landed with a thud and seemed kind of dazed as he managed to pick himself up from the ground and stagger off, putting a hand to his head like he could massage the fog out of it.

My turn to get out. I dangled by my fingertips from the window ledge and tried to let myself down as easy as possible. My height and the two unconscious men piled up beneath me helped shorten the distance. Maybe I wouldn't tell them about the part where I stepped on them a few times trying to get my balance and make it back to solid ground.

My bad!

I grabbed the guy on top by the ankle and started dragging him into the woods. Dead weight was so damned difficult to move.

We were close to the woods, so I only got him to the edge where he wasn't visible from the window any longer. The second guy was slightly lighter but I was so worn out it took longer to drag him to the same spot.

Ghost belly-crawled out of the woods toward me and took the guy's jeans in his mouth, helping me with the weight.

I wondered vaguely what Adak would say if I showed up on his doorstep and asked for a quick healing from one of his witches. The bruises I'd received wouldn't normally be much to deal with, but I was so not looking forward to going up against a jinn in the shape I was in. Not looking forward to it at all.

30

I LOOKED at the small stone blade. It fit easily in my hand, my palm circling round its hilt, the blade about four inches long.

I only had to cut him with it. The stone wouldn't work on most myths, but a jinn was pure magic. Once the blade tasted its blood, he wouldn't be able to fight it. It would pull him in and trap him.

Now I needed to find a way to track the jinn. Easy peasy.

Twenty minutes later, I tried not to look as Hunt handed his brother another chunk of brains. I didn't want to guess what kind they were. Did he kill a deer and feed it to his brother or were these store-bought cow brains or something?

"How did you get him away from them?" I blurted the question without thinking, but I couldn't help but wonder how he'd convinced whatever vampire had turned his brother to give him up.

When a vamp made a male vampire, they usually killed them soon after the turn to harvest the Vamp Dust or let them go zombie as a weapon. Maybe whoever made his brother hadn't wanted him as a weapon or drugs so she'd been happy to give him to his brother.

"Killed her."

Okay, so she hadn't been happy to give him away.

"How old is he?"

Hunt shot his gaze my way. "Sixty-five before they turned him. Been turned for ten years."

"You've had him for ten years?" I couldn't keep the shock from my voice. It was crazy for him to be keeping his brother out here chained up in a shed. Realizing he'd done so for ten years was another thing altogether.

"Three. It took me seven years to track the bitch and get him back."

I didn't have to think about whether I'd spend seven years tracking Dash if someone had done that to him. In a heartbeat, and with no regrets.

I looked around the clearing surrounding Hunt's cabin. Ghost had vanished when we got close but I sensed him waiting in the woods nearby.

"You sent me to take a job from Vivian knowing full well that would have Adeline on my ass."

He gave me a funny look. "I fucking warned you against working as an unregistered here. You ignored me."

Was this guy for real? "You call saying, 'hey don't work unregistered here' sufficient warning that a centuries old vampire would want to skin me for it"?

Not even a flicker of remorse on his face.

I wanted to tell him Vivian had sent me out on some bull-shit made up case, but I hadn't taken care of that binding Vivian had put on me when she hired me. If I talked, I'd lose flesh and bone.

"I'm going after the monster who killed the kid and you're going to help."

Hunt turned to me, wiping the brain remnants on his pants in slow deliberate movements. Would his brother know the difference between the brains he was supposed to eat and the ones on Hunt's pants?

He led his brother back into the shed, taking the time to secure him and the door before coming and sitting on his front step.

"And what would that be? That you're going after, I mean."

"A jinn."

He was shaking his head. "I can't track a jinn. They don't have any odor."

I nodded. "The family he's chasing—one of them is a chimera. Those things stink to high heaven. You can track that."

"And you have money to pay me for this?"

"He dragged a young boy from his bed and slaughtered him in his front yard. He's stalking the family now, including the other young boy, and he's not being careful about the damage he's leaving in his wake. You must have heard about the fires all over the city."

He was unapologetic. "I'm not a bleeding heart and you shouldn't be either. I work for money. That's it. Take a lesson from it, kid."

The fact he was even willing to track for money at all was surprising. Most shifters would take offense at the suggestion they use their skills like a search dog. Hunt wasn't most shifters.

I wasn't going to give up. "Someone tried to make it look like a zombie killed the kid in a rage." I clenched my fingers. It skirted the facts of the case Vivian had hired me for, so I figured I should be safe.

When no body parts fell to the ground, I went on. "I can pay you seventy-five. It's all I've got."

He snorted his response.

I stayed still, not raising my offer. I could wait him out. I didn't look toward the shed where his brother was. I'd told him someone had tried to frame a zombie and that was either enough for him to want to help, or it wasn't.

Long minutes passed before Hunt spoke. "A hundred. And I'll track it but I ain't getting in on this fight. When I find the chimera, whether the jinn's there or not, you're on your own."

I didn't expect anything different. Who would go up against a jinn if they didn't have to? For that matter, even just facing a chimera who felt cornered was risky as hell. Most people wouldn't want any part in that.

I nodded. "Done." I glanced toward the shed. His brother seemed quiet in there. It still boggled my mind how he convinced his brother to stay in the flimsy shed. From what I'd seen of zombies, the chain on the outside would only serve to keep other people out of the shed, not to keep his brother in.

I tipped my head toward the shed. "What's your brother's name?"

Distrust shone in Hunt's eyes but he answered. "Forest."

That was a hell of a name for a zombie.

It also made it a little harder to think of him as an abomination. That's what vampires and zombies were, though. To create one, a vampire had to drain all the blood from a human before replacing it with the blood of the vampire creating it. With it, all humanity left, leaving behind a creature. Nothing more, nothing less.

I looked up at the late morning sun. "Can we go now? There was another fire a couple of hours ago not far from here. We can use that as a starting spot for catching the chimera's scent."

Hunt didn't answer me. He was busy looking past me into the woods behind us. I put a hand to one of my knives and spun.

"He yours?" Hunt asked just as I spotted Ghost wriggling at me from along the tree line.

Ghost scooted forward in a half crouch like he might lay and flip to his side to show his belly at any moment.

I whistled and he doubled his speed, coming to my leg and pressing against me, not stopping the wriggle as he ran. Honestly, sometimes I wasn't sure how he did it.

"If you could teach him not to look so submissive, he might be some use to you."

I turned to glare at Hunt but he raised his arms just as I'd done minutes before.

"Sorry, didn't mean any offense. He's a great dog. A real asset to your team."

31

In his own way, Ghost was a help. I might even go so far as to say asset. I couldn't keep up with Hunt in his wolf form and once he shifted and caught the musky scent of the chimera, the giant of a wolf shifter moved fast.

Ghost circled back to me again and again, making sure I didn't lose sight of Hunt. If I'd been able to communicate with Ghost, I could have asked him to hunt the chimera for me. Maybe over time, he would realize what Hunt was doing in cases like this and I'd be able to get Ghost to do the tracking.

For now, he kept what I always thought of as his goofy smile on his face, tongue lolling, as he circled back to me over and over.

We were entering an area on the east side of town that looked abandoned. There were old warehouses whose roofs probably wouldn't do much to protect if rain came. Still, I could feel eyes on us as we entered the area. There must be homeless people using the spaces for the little shelter they could offer.

I watched as Hunt seemed to move in a cone, going one way for a bit before stopping and turning back. He zigged and zagged, with each swing back and forth getting shorter and shorter until he reached the point of the cone. He stopped in front of a dark gray warehouse and shifted to his human form.

He jerked his chin at the building. "In there."

He wasn't kidding when he said he didn't have a bleeding heart. He took his money and walked away. I looked at Ghost and he looked back at me, as if to ask, "what next?"

So I went in, Ghost on my heels. When I entered the building through the broken door to the left, I didn't need a wolf's nose to smell the chimera. That boy was stressed, and let me tell you, a stressed chimera is a rank chimera.

I stopped just inside the door and held my hands up in front of me. I hadn't spotted him yet, but something told me the chimera was watching every move I made and I was betting he had little tolerance for anyone coming into his hidey hole.

"I'm here to help. My name is Roxie Andrews and I'm tracking the jinn who's coming after your family."

I didn't tell them that I was helping them because my precog Mom left a note saying I'd need them someday. That would just get weird.

A low growl reverberated from the end of the hallway and an enormous beast padded into view. Lord, he took over that space, his lion head with goat horns filling it. To say he had the body of a goat wasn't entirely accurate. I mean, sure, it was shaped like a goat but I'd never seen a goat with haunches the size of a mid-sized truck. And don't get me started on the snake head tail. The black scales seemed covered in a light sheen of gold but it was the red eyes that really topped off the whole look.

To have an animal hiss and growl at me at the same time was just wrong. I held up my hands to show him I meant no harm.

"I promise, I'm only here to help. This thing is wreaking havoc on the city. We need to stop it. Not to mention, I don't take too well to anything that's going after innocent kids."

As I said the words, I knew how true they were. The kid the jinn dragged from his bed and slaughtered could have been my brother, the way we lived under the shadow of Isle and the Illieri coming after us.

Not that she would have killed Dash. She would have killed me and our mom and then taken Dash back to the people who created him. He was a tool to them in their crusade. Nothing more.

I wasn't aware a chimera could speak in its animal form, but he introduced me to that fact with a voice that was all growl. "People lie. Why should I believe you? Why should I put my trust in you? Put my family's lives in your hands?"

Well, damn. I didn't have an answer for him. Except to tell him the truth. "I can't tell you anything that will convince you. I can only show you."

His nostrils flared and he cocked his head. "You're about to get your shot, human."

The word human was a curse on his lips, but I didn't have time to think about that. Within seconds, I could feel the heat and hear the silence. That kind of silence always meant you were well past shit's creek and there wasn't a damned paddle for miles. Not even a twig you could use to steer.

The chimera tipped his head back and in a voice that echoed through the building, cried, "I am here, jinn. Come and meet your fate."

Did he really think he could defeat this thing on his own?

Maybe to him, I was an annoyance. Or maybe, he was scared spitless for his family and was doing the best he could to draw the jinn to him while his wife and kid got out of its path. It's what Mom had done for us when Isle found us. It's what I would do if I was protecting Dash.

There was no telling if his wife and child were hiding or if he'd told them to run. It didn't matter. He and I were going to take this thing on. If it defeated us, it would find the family one way or the other. There would be no one left to stop it.

I knelt at Ghost's side. "I need you to hide, buddy."

He whined and pressed his head into my stomach.

"Sorry, but it has to be this way. This thing is dangerous." I pushed him toward the back of the hall where a stack of old furniture littered the space. "Get yourself under something and don't come out until I come for you."

His head stayed down as he did as I said.

The air filled with heat and sweat broke out across my skin.

The chimera spoke in the silence, this time his voice a low whisper instead of the roar from moments before.

"You'll make a nice appetizer for him, at least. I'll take anything that will give my family more time to get away. Even if that is nothing more than a small morsel of meat he has to chew through to get to me."

Yippee. He'd just equated me to a pig in a blanket.

My left hand went to one of the steel knives on my hip, the one with the channel of silver running through the metal to weaken any opponents who were sensitive to silver. I didn't know if anything other than the vessel would weaken this thing, but I wanted the silver just in case.

My right hand went to the vessel secured at the small of my back. I just needed this thing to get close enough to nick it with the vessel and we were good to go.

Assuming I could do that without dying.

The door I'd just come through slammed open, the hinges giving up the fight as it hit the wall and slumped to the floor.

The form in the doorway was human shaped. Ish. I mean, it had arms and legs and a head.

It was tall, bending more than a little to come through the doorway.

If molten lava could take form and walk, this was it. It was disturbing the way it had no smell and no smoke. Of course, as it stood in the doorway, the wood on either side of it and beneath its feet began to scorch and smolder. If it stood still much longer, we'd have smoke and fire soon enough.

The jinn seemed to grin as he pulled gleaming blades from nowhere. I wondered briefly if the knives would be hot and cauterize any wound they made but dismissed the thought.

I'd seen the blood on the lawn where he killed the boy. Maybe he could control whether he heated something he was holding or not. He hadn't set the kid's house on fire when he grabbed him from his bedroom so he must be able to control it.

Of course, that meant he was purposely burning us to the ground.

I opened my mouth to say something I'm sure would have been witty, but before I could, he was barreling into me. I don't think I even blinked before I had the wind knocked out of me as I hit the floor. Normally I would breathe out on the way down to keep that from happening, but he was too damned fast. There was no time to react.

My knife and the vessel went flying, but I was more distracted by the fact that I couldn't get air into my lungs. I watched in horror as I tried to right my failing airways while the jinn went after the chimera. I guess he thought I was finished.

I forced my lungs to exhale knowing that would reset my breathing when all my body thought I should do was gulp for air.

The chimera roared but it didn't faze the jinn at all. As the jinn tried to slash the chimera's face, the chimera dodged before retaliating with powerful jaws. While neither was really doing damage, they were managing to thwart the other in the process.

The jinn got a good strike in on the chimera, putting a nasty gash in the side of his face. The roar from the injured beast was deafening.

I couldn't wait any longer. I grabbed a knife from my hip and threw it at the jinn. I hit my mark and the knife stuck in its back, but it was like it didn't even notice. The knife was no more than a mosquito bite to this thing and I watched as it melted into him, becoming part of the endless fire. This was going to be harder than I thought.

A quick look around didn't reveal where the vessel might have gone and the jinn was grabbing the chimera with fiery hands as the poor beast bellowed in agony. No way in hell I'd leave him to fight the jinn on his own.

I ran full tilt at the jinn, leaping into the air to strike at him with my boots to his side. I managed to knock him away from the chimera for just a moment.

The chimera took the opportunity to bite at the jinn, sinking its teeth into its arm and I heard the jinn's howl this time. The sound was ear-splitting. I wouldn't be at all surprised to find blood dripping from my ears.

The chimera swung his head and ripped at the arm, spraying bright orange blood everywhere as though he'd torn something vital, but the jinn recovered quickly. He continued to bleed some but this thing was clearly not your average myth. Did it feel no pain? Was it just screaming in anger at getting bitten?

Or was the scream a defense mechanism meant to disable his opponents with the piercing sound? I didn't really have time to debate the reasons. I wanted that damned vessel. I worked hard to get that thing and now would be a really fucking nice time to have it.

I was gearing up to jump into the fray when the jinn wrapped its arms around itself and started to shake.

Had the chimera really hurt it? I wanted to watch what it was doing, but I also needed to find the vessel. I tried to keep one eye on the two of them while looking around, but a loud popping noise and scorching heat wave halted all plans.

The force of the surge blew me backwards. This had to be what being inside a microwave felt like.

I could feel blisters forming on my skin, the heat and pain fueling my anger. This thing had to die.

The chimera had gone down but was struggling back to his feet now. The look on his face said he was as pissed as I was. He turned his back on the jinn, wrapping his snake tail around it, pinning its arms. He howled in pain and I would guess the Jinn's heat was searing through him, but he continued to squeeze.

He was willing to die for his family.

I leapt toward them, leading with my elbow and landing a blow to the side of the jinn's head. I didn't know how the chimera was holding on. Just that small contact with my skin had me reeling back.

The small hit burned my skin badly and it took a lot to swallow down the pain and strike him again. I went for the head, this time leading with my fist. I hit him again and again before turning to search for the vessel. We weren't going to be able to take this thing down without it. I needed the magic it would bring to this fight and I needed it now.

Mom's words echoed in my head. "Nobody ever looks up when they're looking for something."

I shot my gaze toward the ceiling and there it was, stuck into the stained ceiling tiles.

That's when I heard the sizzle. The jinn was burning through the chimera's tail.

He'd be burned alive. I figured he would have to trust me since we had a common enemy and I pulled two knives from my hip as I ran at them. I spun and landed backwards, cowgirl style, on the chimera's back, stabbing the knives into the jinn's eyes. I continued to push and twist as the jinn tried to get away.

The jinn exploded with fire and rage, severing the snake tail from the chimera. The jinn backed up, grabbing at his face, screeching as he plunged the knives deep into his eye sockets where they melted like the one in his back had.

Unlike the knife to his back earlier, these seemed to do some damage to his eyes.

The chimera began to howl and buck at the pain of losing his tail. I held on for dear life, grabbing fur to try to keep from flying off. The next time he bucked to the right, I let go, reaching as he sent me flying right by the vessel. I plucked it out of the ceiling before beginning my way down to the very hard ground.

I heard the crunch before I felt the pain. My left knee was in more pieces now than it was just seconds ago. Pain shot through my leg and then disappeared, I guess due to shock and adrenaline.

I felt the weight of the vessel in my hand. It was time to end this. If I didn't, I doubted I'd be walking out of here alive.

It would help if I could put my weight on both legs, but I'd make do with one. The jinn was wrapping its arms around itself again.

Oh, hell no. We were not going to let him radiate us again.

Too bad I couldn't really move. The chimera turned, using his giant body to slam the jinn into the wall, breaking whatever concentration the fire creature had and giving me seconds to act.

But that only stopped the shockwave. The jinn recovered quickly, slamming into the chimera's shoulder. The chimera hit the ground with a thud that rattled the building. He was still breathing, but he was hanging on by a thread.

And now the walking inferno was coming at me.

I gripped the vessel, ready to stab this thing when it came at me.

He stopped, spotting the stone knife, clearly recognizing what it was.

Great. Brawn and brains on this one. I always preferred it when it was one or the other.

My other hand started to tingle and relief ran through me as my bo shot out of nowhere. I put one end of the staff on the ground to hold myself up as I turned the vessel in my hand, lining the blade up against my forearm in a proper knife hold. It was time to end this. I only needed to give the stone knife a small taste of this thing's blood and this fight was over.

I crouched waiting for him to come play. Something told me the jinn couldn't resist the invitation and I was just stupid enough to let this thing get close enough to burn me alive if that meant getting the slice of him I needed to activate the vessel.

A deafening crack from the roof had us both looking up. A section of the ceiling ripped away into the sky, held by powerful dragon jaws and talons. Adak and several others swooped down from above.

I ignored them and turned to the jinn. I was so damned close. All I needed was a few more seconds and this would be over. I was so close.

It wasn't going to happen. The jinn must have decided there were too many to take on. He cranked up the fire, getting so hot he turned to molten lava in front of me.

I raised my arm to shield myself from the heat. I couldn't get close to it now. The jinn turned and ran, reaching out with its flames as it passed the back wall, setting it on fire.

Adak barreled toward it, but the thing was too fast. In seconds, the wall crumbled and the jinn escaped like the barrier was wet tissue paper. Adak's dragons closed in on it, giving chase and smothering it with the fire that shot from their mouths, but the jinn only grew as it raced away from their flames and out of sight.

There was a moment of stunned silence as Adak landed and shifted in a single breath.

My eyes took in the charred remains of the side of the building, then landed on Adak's gaze.

"What the hell are you doing?" I yelled this at the same time as his holiness the royal alpha yelled almost the same words.

Screw him, he owed me answers.

He stalked toward me and tried to use his height to intimidate.

Good luck with that. I grew up with a woman who frightened battled hardened warriors on her meekest of days. And she'd done a hell of a lot more to me than mere intimidation tactics during our training sessions.

I growled at him. "I had him where I needed him. What the hell were you thinking barging in here like that?"

Adak leaned in, getting right in my face. "Yeah, that looked like a brilliantly conceived, dazzlingly executed battle plan. Let him squash you like a bug. Well done."

"It was, you idiot. I have a vessel. All I needed to do was nick him with it and I would have if you'd let him keep coming at me!"

"So your plan was to let him kill you and hope he stubbed his big toe on the vessel in the process?"

Dragons were too damned arrogant. Arrogant and cocky and pushy as all hell.

I elbowed him in the chest and was happy to see he moved a hair in response. A minuscule hair but a hair, nonetheless. "I had it covered and now I need to trap him all over again."

If I was honest, I was starting to feel the pain of my injuries. I didn't want to look to see how badly burned I was.

Damn, I forgot the chimera! I hobbled toward the hallway where I'd last seen him. The jinn burned his snake tail right off him and he hadn't looked like he would survive.

He was crumpled in a heap in the hallway, slumped against

the wall. His tail lay a foot from his body. The rest of him was nearly one large swath of seared flesh.

I tried to fall to my knees beside him, but pain raged through one of my legs at the motion. I ended up sort of slumping down to one side instead. My legs were in bad shape and they weren't going to hold back on telling me that anymore.

"Adak!" I croaked out. "Did you bring healers?" I'd figure out how to pay for this later. I told the chimera I'd stand with him and now he was nearly dead.

The dragon was behind me in seconds and I heard others come up with him.

"Move." His command was brusque, but I didn't care.

The chimera was battling to take even the smallest of breaths, wild eyes finding me and locking on.

Some help I'd been.

"We always bring healers," Adak said, his voice low as seven of his witches moved in to crouch over the Chimera. I was appalled to see them drag his lifeless tail over to him but when they lined it up with the stump, I couldn't look away.

The witches were scribbling their runes. They wrapped the spells around the tail as the beast panted, then they started to chant.

I'd heard of some miraculous healings before, but these guys thought they could reattach body parts.

Wind gusted through the building, whipping along the hallway and settling over the chimera and the healers. It wound through the broken pieces of the beast as the witches kept up their chanting.

Sweat covered the brow of nearly all of the witches and they raised their voices, the magic moving from a hum to a pulsing wash of power.

In minutes, his body was whole. Seconds after that, magic

swirled around him and his human form lay on the ground. He blinked open crystal blue eyes and met mine.

Before I could say anything, Adak spoke.

"She's next," he ordered and I looked around to see who he was talking about.

The healers were looking at me.

I looked down at myself and realized I was doing worse than I'd thought. My legs had blistered and burned with lacerations sprinkled in the mix for shits and giggles, and my knee was blown up big as a balloon.

My arms, though … those were numb. The flesh on my forearms was nothing but white char and my bones were exposed in some places. My fingers were much the same.

As soon as the realization hit me, I turned and threw up, losing every last bit of the contents of my stomach.

Thankfully, I'd had the wherewithal to turn away from Adak instead of puking on his shoes.

Ghost came out then, ignoring my instruction to wait until I came to get him. He was by my side in a heartbeat, whimpering his support.

The healers ignored the pretty picture I'd just painted on the floor and stood on either side of me, wrapping their thin paper stuff over all parts of my body.

Their lips moved in a chant as their hands hovered over my arms. The strong wind came again and I began to feel the prickling burn of the magic.

This time, it wasn't just a prickle. It grew and swelled, and with it the pain grew as searing heat burned through me again. It hurt like a bitch, flooding me with an agonizing ache that had me gritting my teeth as I screamed and tried not to throw up again.

And then it was gone. The ache, the charred skin, the stench of cooked flesh. They'd healed me completely after healing the chimera's serious injuries.

They might have been sweating a little but I got the sense they could have kept right on going. I don't think I'd truly realized the raw power of the members of Adak's pack before.

He stepped in, growling as he did. "Let us handle the jinn. That's payment enough."

Oh hell, no he didn't. I liked it when people underestimated me in a fight. I didn't like it when they treated me like a toddler after seeing what I was capable of. I opened my mouth to argue, but he didn't stick around for it.

Those eyes stayed on me as he raised his voice and called to his pack. "Nova Force, move out."

It was an order and they followed without comment or argument. I almost had to laugh at the immediate obedience he was used to, as his people shifted out of their human forms and witches and wolves hopped onto the backs of their dragons.

Adak shot into the air and was gone from sight faster than I could blink.

And it was a full minute before I realized that he hadn't shifted into a dragon before leaving the ground.

If I had to describe what happened, I would say he leapt into the air as a man and in the blink of an eye wings formed to shove the air southward as a dragon emerged. It was sure as hell nothing I'd ever seen a dragon shifter do. Ever.

There was a hell of a lot more to Adak and his Nova Force than met the eye. A hell of a lot.

32

Roxie

"What now?"

I looked over at the chimera—now a man with red hair and bright blue eyes. He was younger than I'd imagined him. Maybe in his early twenties, if that.

"Now," I said, looking down at the vessel I'd recovered and now palmed, "we figure out how to cut that asshole with this."

The look I got was dubious at best. "With a stone knife?"

"It's not just a stone knife. It's a vessel. Uh, basically a magic stone knife. If we can even nick him with it, the knife will suck him into it and trap him. Then we can destroy the knife."

"I'm Cristiano." He held out his hand. I guess I'd earned his trust.

I looked at the pale freckled skin for a minute before taking it and shaking once. His name didn't match his looks, which I would guess were Scottish.

"Roxie," I said. I looked around the destroyed space. "We

need to get your family away from this fight and then figure out a way to lure him out."

"He can scent them. I don't know how to hide them from that."

I thought for a minute. "I do. We need a magic fold."

Cristiano snorted. "Yeah, lemme just run on out and find one. Maybe the corner store is having a sale."

"Nah, they're sold out. But I happen to have one."

He studied me for a minute before turning and waving for me to follow him. Ghost followed as we went down the hallway I'd first found Cristiano in and through a series of doors and turns before he stopped in front of a large metal filing cabinet.

The floor objected to the movement, letting out a screeching howl, but it gave up its secrets just the same.

On the floor beneath the cabinet was a trap door. Cristiano lifted it and a moment later I watched as his wife and child came up through the door.

She was small and slim, with white-blonde hair and green eyes that looked like the moss on trees deep in the woods. Her son looked just like her and I wondered if his brother had looked the same before the jinn gutted him.

The woman's eyes found me and she flew to Cristiano's side, pulling her son along with her, fear cutting her face.

"She's okay," Cristiano said, his arms going around her and their son. "She's with us. We're going to get you guys to a magic fold and hide you."

Ghost whined and went to the boy. I saw the kid run his hand over Ghost's back and Ghost didn't wink out of existence. Good. Maybe Ghost could keep the boy calm.

Cristiano's wife looked up at him with trust in her eyes.

"This is Roxie," the chimera said. "Roxie, this is Mira and Kallum."

I nodded but looked over my shoulder. "We should move now while we can."

Mira stepped away from Cristiano as he reached down into the hole they'd come out of to lift a huge backpack as though it weighed nothing, even though the thing had so much strapped to it, it must be eighty pounds. He slung it over a shoulder and put a hand on Kallum, leading the boy as we turned to head out of the warehouse.

They were quiet as I got them all loaded into my car and I realized they hadn't even had the chance to mourn their other son. They hadn't been able to deal with the horror of that stolen life. Instead, they were on the run themselves, trying to make sure the jinn didn't get Kallum.

When I got us onto Capital of Texas Highway, I cleared my throat. "What does the jinn want with you?" I asked Cristiano quietly. I saw Mira blanch in the backseat and tug her son closer to her, but knowing what was going on might help us figure out how to lure this guy in.

"It's not me he's after," Cristiano said just as quietly, checking on the passengers in the back. Kallum had closed his eyes and leaned on his mother, his breathing evening out with the heavy steadiness of sleep. "I met Mira and the boys when I was a guard at a vegetable plantation."

My eyes shot to him. I should have guessed the kids weren't his since he was a Chimera and neither kid showed any signs of that heritage, but he sure as hell treated Kallum like he was his from the little I'd seen.

As if reading my mind, he tilted his chin up. "They're mine. I don't need my blood running through their veins to prove it."

I shook my head. "You don't need to tell me. My brother and I don't share blood, but that doesn't change who he is."

He seemed to take that assurance and kept going. "Mira is a garden nypmh."

I nodded. I'd already figured that out.

His voice took on a hard, unyielding edge. "They kept her there. She and the boys were prisoners. Mira was forced to use her magic to make sure the vegetable crops don't die when the magic burns come."

I cursed. Hell, I should have figured it was something like that when I realized she was a garden nymph. The magic burns were freaking everyone out. Not only did they harm crops and raise food prices, there were scientists saying if we continued to lose plant life like we were, it would speed up global warming to levels we couldn't hope to undo.

But still, I hadn't heard of companies keeping people as slaves for that before. "Why aren't they paying a coven to handle that like most companies do?"

His face twisted into a sneer. "Because Mira can single-handedly halt the effects of a magic burn on all their crops at once. She's powerful. And the boys are—"

He stopped and swallowed hard and I knew he had to be thinking about the fact that they only had one son left now. That Jake wasn't coming back to them.

"There was a new partner in the plantation who was talking about changing things. I never met him, but I heard talk. He knew the boys were turning out to be as powerful as she was and started talking about separating them. Sending them to other plantations to expand operations. I was already trying to get her and the boys out of there, but when this new guy got involved, we had to act fast. I couldn't let them take the boys and risk not being able to find them."

I didn't handle emotion like this well. I cleared my throat. "And they were willing to sacrifice Jake to show her what will happen if she doesn't come back. If she doesn't fall in line."

He gave a jerky nod.

Still, I wondered why they would sacrifice one of the boys if they were worth all that? Why not grab the boys and hold them until Mira cooperated? And why a jinn? Was he simply a hired mercenary the vegetable growers had sent? There was something I was missing here.

I pulled into the long drive that would lead to my cabin and blew out a breath. "I have a small magic fold at the back of my cabin." I didn't tell him I had planned to save enough money to have the fold stretched so I could use it as a home for myself someday.

No point in telling him that now. He and his family needed it more than I did.

"It's not much but you can hide there. I've got a tent in my trunk that might fit in the fold."

He looked around as I pulled into the clearing outside my cabin. With half the woods on the side taken out from the tornadoes Gransen's little buddies had thrown at me and the magic burn marks that riddled the woods, the place wasn't much to look at for the moment.

I shut the engine and looked at him. "We'll get your family hidden in the fold and then I'll figure out how to track the jinn again."

I grinned the kind of toothy grin that was more a display of teeth than a true smile.

He gave me the same smile right back.

33

Roxie

Once again, I drove toward town. Cristiano, Mira, and Kallum were tucked into the fold where they'd be safe, but I needed to think.

Driving cleared my head. I was still trying to figure out a lot of things. Like why the jinn was involved in this and why the plantation owners would have allowed it to kill one of Mira's sons. If what Cristiano said was true, they would have been able to use him on another plantation to make a ton of money. Or sell him.

Why did they let the jinn kill him to send a message?

I kept one hand on the wheel and one on Ghost in the passenger seat beside me. My hand found the rough spots on his shoulders. I could swear they were getting worse, spreading and covering more of his skin. Maybe it was a rash not scratches.

Shit, I should get him to a vet to make sure they weren't

something to worry about. Not that he acted sick or in pain. He didn't mind at all when I touched the area.

I pulled onto the highway, mulling over everything that had happened from the minute Dash and I had hit town to the battle with the jinn.

If my hand slowed on Ghost, he pushed that rock head of his under it to get it moving again. When he wasn't reminding me to pet him, he snuffled, small snores coming out as he slept.

Twenty minutes later, I realized I had brought myself to south Austin. I was down the street from the hedge witch's house.

What the hell was my subconscious trying to tell me?

Probably that I'd never confronted her and I was no closer to figuring out how she was tied into all of this. Why did she have a vessel? That seemed a little convenient with a jinn terrorizing the city.

At the very least, I should have a chat with the hedge and convince her to release me from the binding. In a friendly way, of course.

I parked and turned to Ghost, who now sat up in the passenger seat, looking for all the world like a co-pilot watching the road like he might take over driving any minute.

"Stay here, buddy. If I'm not back in a few hours, can you find your way up to Dash?"

He whined and licked my hand. That was as good of a "yes" as I was going to get. I left a window down, both so he could get air and so he could get himself out if I didn't come back or it got too hot.

Dash was miles away, but Ghost had followed us from Colorado to Austin somehow, so I was banking on him be able to locate him.

He whined and flapped his tail a few times at me, but I shook my head. "I need you to stay out of this, buddy. I have to know you're safe."

More whining, but I kissed the top of his head and gave him a stern look. "Do not follow me, mister. I'll ground you for a month. No snacky snacks."

A snacky snack was anything edible to him, and that covered a lot. The dog would eat just about anything.

I moved around to the back of the house, keeping myself alert for wards and traps in case she'd decided to beef up security after my last visit.

As I came up along the back corner of the house, I felt the remnants of a ward, as if its tattered pieces still floated on the wind. That didn't bode well for Vivian.

I stilled and listened, waiting for any sign of a disturbance. Nothing outside the house, but inside, I heard voices.

Gransen.

Had he been the one to blow through her ward?

I moved on silent feet to a spot that let me see into the den at the back of the house.

Gransen stood over Vivian, six of his men filling the space around them, making sure she didn't get away.

I checked the area around me again. I was alone out here.

"I didn't hire her to go after your jinn," Vivian said, sounding a little like an insolent child. "I hired her to kill a zombie."

Great. I was the topic of conversation for this meeting. That didn't bode well.

Gransen's brows rose and he looked like a cat who'd caught a mouse and knew it could play for hours. "My, my. Isn't that a coincidence since I hired you to make it look like the Connor boy had been killed by a zombie? Did you try to turn my project into your own?"

Vivian's eyes flashed but she managed to look like she was trying at meek and submissive for him at the same time. Neat trick.

My mind raced as I took in what he'd just said. He hired

Vivian to make the police think it was a zombie killing. She must be damned good at illusion magic, then. Had she shown me an illusion of an empty house when I came looking for her before?

"I had no choice," she cried. "That whore Dominica has been holding me hostage for years. I had to get out of her grip!"

If Gransen knew what she was talking about, he didn't show it. I sure as hell didn't have a clue.

"You and Dominica are tight. Why would you cross her?" Gransen grilled her.

Vivian shook her head so violently I thought she might snap her own neck before Gransen had the chance.

"A lie. She pretended to be my friend. Ten years ago, she discovered my longevity anchor and she's held it over me, making me use all my power to create illusions for the club patrons night after night like I'm some kind of circus freak. It was beneath me!"

I remembered someone mentioning a nightclub where patrons could get an illusion to make them look and feel like whatever they wanted to be.

It made sense that Vivian would feel trapped if this Dominica chick had the anchor that held Vivian's longevity spells. If that was destroyed, she would age to her true age in a matter of seconds.

Gransen began to pace, tapping his chin as though he were engaging in a level of thought I wasn't honestly sure he was capable of.

"It's a problem when someone has your anchor." He turned to face the hedge witch again, who was nodding at him.

He sighed an over-the-top sigh. "But to cross me. That was stupid, Viv. Monumentally stupid."

"I just wanted my anchor back!" Vivian cried.

Gransen paused and looked at her. "You mean this?"

He pulled a necklace with a deep purple gemstone from his

pocket and I watched as Vivian's face blanched. She looked as though she'd begun aging already and the anchor was still intact.

He held the necklace aloft and flicked the purple stone with his finger. "Dominica was loath to release it to me since she'll need to find a new gimmick for her club without her illusionist, but she's smart enough to know who to respect."

He looked down at her, his voice going dangerously quiet. "Tell me, where is my vessel?"

Vivian moaned and bent double, clutching her hands together in a silent plea.

Well damn, I'd stolen the vessel she'd presumably been holding onto for Gransen. He must have given her the jinn to set on Mira and her kids.

I might feel bad if she wasn't clearly involved in the murder of a child. I didn't have pity for anyone messed up in something like that.

Gransen was unmoved. He dropped the stone to the floor and put his boot on it. "You know that my plans relied on everyone believing the boy was dead, but you hired a dagger and sent her sniffing around the crime scene?"

It took me several seconds to process what he'd said, but when it hit me, it hit hard. If his plans relied on people believing the boy was dead, that meant he wasn't, right?

Jake Connor wasn't dead!

I didn't have time to sit with that long.

Vivian shrieked. "I only sent her so she'd kill Dominica's zombie for me. She was never supposed to investigate the child's death!"

"Then I guess that means your illusion wasn't good enough. You've known me long enough to know I don't tolerate failure." Gransen raised his boot and brought it down, crushing her anchor under his heel.

The scream that erupted from Vivian wasn't one of anger or

rage or promised retribution. It was desperation and panic. It was defeat.

The skin on her face began to sag and go sallow and gray. Her hair turned gray, then white, chunks of it falling to the floor.

Vivian scrambled for the hair with hands that could have been those of a hundred-year-old woman. She cried out as she collected the hair, holding it close to her chest.

Her face was skeletal, the skin hanging from sunken cheeks and hollow eyes. She looked down at her hands, now crumbling in on themselves, flesh and bone turning to dust and falling to the floor.

Her wailing ceased and a long hollow breath came, wheezing out of her cadaverous chest until it was no more. Until she was no more.

With a last whoosh, the dust that had been a person moments before, fell and blew across the floor.

34

I LEFT the way I'd come, watching for any of Gransen's men. The last thing I needed was for Gransen or his men to realize I'd just witnessed that. I wasn't stupid. I needed backup if I was going to go after the kid.

And I was going to go after the kid. If Jake really was alive, what Cristiano had feared could come true. Gransen could sell him or move him to another plantation and if that happened, finding him might not be possible.

Our best shot at saving that kid was to go after him right now before Gransen had a chance to do anything with him.

Ghost stood up when I approached, watching me through the window.

"Hey boy." I rubbed his head when I got in before starting the car and beating it the hell out of there.

With Vivian dead, I didn't have to worry about the binding she'd put on me.

I drove toward the huge old church Gransen used as his

base. Myths seemed to think it was fucking hysterical to use human churches for houses, lairs, and coven centers.

Gransen's church was an enormous building with a tall steeple tower that I was guessing they used as a launchpad to take flight.

I couldn't call Cristiano. He and his family were hiding in the fold and I didn't have his phone number. Not to mention, I didn't want to get his hopes up until I knew Jake was alive and here.

If I called him and he came down here, the jinn would be on his trail in a heartbeat and I'd be dealing with the jinn and Gransen.

There was always Officer Adams, but she'd said herself her department wasn't really in charge in this city. I didn't know if she could raise a team of officers strong enough to take on Gransen. Officers who weren't on his payroll.

If I was one of Adeline's daggers, I could theoretically call for backup from other daggers, but with the balance of power in Austin the way it was, would she have some rule where her daggers couldn't interfere with Gransen and his people?

All of this brought me down to the only other person I could call, and the only one who made any sense.

I dialed Adak's phone as I pulled past Gransen's church and parked a block away down an alley.

"What's wrong?" Adak's voice was all concern, so I guess he was done being mad at me.

I guess I was done being mad at him if I was calling him for backup.

"I think Jake Connor is alive and Gransen has him."

I gave him a few beats before filling him in on the whole story despite the utter silence on the other end of the line.

"We'll be right there."

He disconnected before I could answer. I wanted to creep around the backside of Gransen's building and see if I could spot the kid, but I wasn't that stupid. It wasn't like they'd have him sitting at the kitchen table in plain view of the window.

I'd wait until Adak's people got there and we could take on Gransen and his men together.

Ghost stood in his seat and whined, looking toward the church. I was keeping my eyes on the road behind us and the sky above us. I didn't want Gransen to stumble on us waiting here when he came back from his morning of killing those who crossed him.

Ghost barked, just a single bark, eyes locked on the church. We could only see the steeple, but he was looking right toward the block where the church was located, as though he knew something I didn't know.

Fantastic. Love it when that happened.

"What is it?" I resisted the urge to add 'Lassie' to the end of that question.

He whined again, eyes locked onto the same spot.

"Damn." I needed to find out what he was barking at. Which meant I was going to be the stupid woman who went into something before her backup arrived.

Hell, I could at least do a drive-by.

I started my car and pulled out of the alley, turning left to circle the block. I should be able to spot the back of the church and then drive around to see if something was happening out front.

I could spot Gransen's men on the street. They stood out, glaring at the world around them.

A dark gray van stood at the back entrance to the church, idling. I was just in time to see a flicker of white-blond hair on a little body before the door was slammed shut.

I swore a lot. A whole lot.

Then I looked at Ghost as two of Gransen's men got into the front of the van and pulled away.

"Stay here and hide until Adak comes, then lead him to me,

okay?" I had to hope he could use those big brown eyes to convince Adak to follow him. If I wasn't far, he could track me a lot faster than he tracked me from Colorado.

Ghost gave a little rumble and I leaned over to open the door and let him hop out before following the van from a distance.

Adak would be pissed that I'd left without him, but if that was Jake I'd seen in the van, there was no way I was letting him out of my sight.

I stayed a block to two back, sometimes letting the van get ahead of me around a corner before catching up. This would work a lot better if there was more than one of me to coordinate and drop back, but I hadn't figured out how to clone myself yet.

I followed for several miles moving further south of the city, all the while checking the skies to see if my backup had arrived. Where the hell was Adak?

When we got to a more remote area with less traffic, I had to fall back much more, barely keeping the van in sight so they wouldn't see me, though at this point, I might have to give up trying to hide.

If it was a choice between letting them spot me and leaving the kid on his own, I'd choose to go get that kid every time.

I dialed Adak again, putting it on speaker so I could keep driving.

"Adak, did you find Ghost yet?"

I divided my attention between the phone and the road, maneuvering around a broken-down truck on the side of the road.

Whatever Adak said in response was lost when the truck pulled out behind me, the woman who'd been looking under its hood, hopping up onto the back of it as it sped toward me at a too-fast pace.

The truck rammed the back of my car and I swore,

capturing the wheel and keeping myself on the road, but only just.

My phone fell to the floor and I heard Adak doing a little swearing of his own as he called out to me.

Two more trucks pulled out from the side of the road blocking me. I could ram them, which wouldn't do much with my little car. I could swerve off and try to off-road it. Again, not a great idea. Mental note to get a more kick-ass car.

The van I'd been following was too far ahead of me to catch at this point, and I had my hands full. I yelled out my general location and the van description to Adak, hoping he could still hear me as four of what I could only assume were Gransen's men surrounded my car.

One of the assholes grinned the shit-eating kind as he rapped on my window with a weighty fist.

Fuck me.

My odds were bad. They were too close to the car. I should have veered off if for no other reason than to give myself some space. I shoved the car door open as fast and wide as I could and came out throwing punches and knives.

I might have made it. I caught the guy with the grin with an upper cut that wiped the smile off his ugly face.

My bo staff appeared for me almost immediately, which told me just how much trouble I was in. I was able to take down two of the men with my bo, but the sky filled with dragons and this time, they weren't the friendly kind.

Gransen shifted before me, shaking his head.

"Roxie, you really have to learn to keep your nose out of my business. You think I didn't see you watching at Vivian's house?"

Well, yeah, I had thought that.

"My guys have been leading you to where I wanted you this whole time and you followed them like a fucking puppet."

Okay, the man had some valid criticisms there. I tended to

have a blind spot when a kid was in trouble and Gransen had played on that perfectly.

Still, not to be outdone, I gave one final twist of my bo, wrenching it up and cracking him under the chin with it.

I didn't see much after that. Too many of his people were on me. Too many blows. Too much to battle back.

I know I caught at least a few of them with an elbow or a knee but there were spots dancing in my vision and when one of them got his arm around my neck in a lock, there were too many there backing him up for me to get out of it.

Gransen was sporting a gash under his chin when he grinned at me one last time, right before his boot caught up with my skull and I went out.

35

ROXIE

THE MAN HAD A DUNGEON. I don't know why I was surprised by this.

Concrete cells and bars. That counted as a dungeon, right?

I woke up on the cold hard floor with no clue how much time had passed. I hoped not much. I didn't know where we were. I was hoping in whatever place they'd taken Jake to so I still had a shot at finding him and getting him back to his family.

Look at me, all confident I could do jack all as a fucking captive.

I wasn't the only one in here. There were people moaning in the other cells. I strained, listening for the sound of a child, but I was still out of it. My head and ribs ached and I wished I had a good healing witch in the cell with me.

I also had to deal with the small issue of how to get out of here. I was in no condition to fight anyone. Let's hope stealth could win the day until Adak and his people found me.

Ghost would lead him to me. Of that I was sure.

I slid my hand in my boot thanking the fates Gransen's men hadn't found the magic pocket that held the vessel I needed to defeat the jinn.

The pocket also held the most important relics Mom had collected over the years. There were a few gems and bits with various powers. But what I needed now were the four small glass vials held together with a leather strap.

It wasn't easy to part with the treasures. I'd held onto them for a long time. They were part of a stash of a few magical items we'd bought over the years during the flush times, which frankly were outweighed by the not flush times.

I hadn't sold them when things were looking pretty bleak for Dash and I, but if now wasn't the time to use these little guys, I didn't know when would be.

The worms that slid out when I opened two of the vials were slithering gray bits of slime that went from short and fat to long and thin when they stretched, seeking to feed now that the stasis of the magical vials was gone and they were awake.

I could see that the cell bars were iron with a channel of silver running down either side of them. Pricey but worth it since one or the other of the two metals usually weakened myth creatures.

I wouldn't be surprised if the concrete walls had a core of the combination of the two metals to weaken anyone they threw in here. That little effect would be attractive to someone like Gransen.

I cringed as I lifted the nasty little maggots and placed one near the bottom of one bar and the other at the top. If they could eat through the bar, I could slip through the gap it left.

There were two more of the worms in my boot but if I had to use all four to get out of my cell, I'd have no way to get the kid out of his, assuming he was here.

The metal worms wrapped their mushy bodies around the

bar and began to eat. It wasn't like eating with a mouth. They seemed to absorb the metal into them through the surface of what I guess you would describe as their underbelly.

I reached out and grasped the middle of the bar. I didn't want it clattering to the ground when they'd made their way through their meal.

The worms began to glow, giving off a soft blue light. They hadn't come with a set of instructions so I had no idea what would happen next. Here's hoping it wasn't loud.

The place was dark and mostly quiet, save for the groans and snuffles and snorts coming from the cells nearby. I eyed what I could see of the hallway outside my cell. It wasn't much. Were we in some kind of bunker?

"The fuck is that?" I heard from somewhere next to my cell.

Well, shit. There were more murmurs. If these fuckers got me caught I was gonna need to slay the whole fucking lot of them.

I watched as the light of the worms grew brighter and then it stopped. They stopped. They slid to the ground and lay still as I looked at what was left of the bar. They hadn't eaten all the way through it.

Damn, damn, damn.

Maybe they'd rest for a bit and then I could put them back up there to feed again.

Sure, and in the meantime, I'd hope no one came in here and noticed the way the bars had miraculously developed lesions in two spots.

The worms started to writhe and I stepped back. Maybe they were going to have a growth spurt and then need to eat again? I remembered Dash doing that when he was a kid. He'd eat like a fucking beaver going through a tree and then grow an inch or two, before starting the whole thing over again.

No such luck. I watched as the worms' slimy outer skin

started to shed and wet wings unfurled and stretched. Butter-flies. Fucking butterflies?

Within minutes, their wings were dry, revealing a gorgeous shimmering blue sheen on top of silver. Then they were gone, flying through the bars and out of the cell.

Okay, great. So unless I wanted to use the other two worms, I had to get through this bar myself.

I fingered the metal. Less than a pinky's width left on top and bottom. I could break that, right?

Aw hell. Looked like I was going to try, at least.

I took a few steps back and stepped into a side kick, my heel shooting out at the bar.

Fucking troll dicks! That did not work like in the movies. But I think I felt it give a little.

I had to give myself a small pep talk before the next couple of kicks since I knew how much it hurt now, but I kicked again. And again. And again. My heel was going numb and I had almost given up hope when my foot went through the target, sending the bar flying across the hallway with a loud clattering noise.

After squeezing between the bars, I limped over to where it had fallen, clenching my jaw against the pain shooting up my leg.

I picked up the bar and hefted it in my hand, waiting to see if the noise I'd made would bring guards running. All around me, people called out for me to take them with me.

The man in the cell next to me reached his arm out toward me, but I pulled away from him. I was here for one person and that was Jake.

People reached for me as I scanned the cells looking for the boy. Some looked like they deserved to be there. Hard eyes and scars that proved they weren't nice people. But others looked like they'd just run up against Gransen for some reason or another and landed here.

One woman watched me with haunted eyes as I limped along, my foot throbbing in pain. She wore an apron that looked like Gransen's henchmen grabbed her from her kitchen or a bakery, but the fabric was old and dingy. How long had she been there?

The crying I heard as I neared the end of the row of cells was distinctly child-like. I rushed to the cell and found Jake, his face blotchy and his green eyes a mask of fear and panic.

"Hey kid, I'm going to get you out of here." I reached into my boot for the other worms and worked the tops off as Jake looked at me, wary hope on his face.

"Did my mom send you?"

I smiled, half lying to the kid since his parents didn't know I was here. "Her and Cristiano, and your brother, too. Kallum's been missing you a lot." I looked at the bars. "My little worm buddies are gonna do their thing here and eat through the bars."

I didn't get specific about the fact they would only get part of the way through it and I'd need to try to use what was likely my now broken foot to get the bar out. Maybe these little guys would be hungrier than the others?

The worms started to do their thing as angry shouts came from the other prisoners. Did they think I could help them if they drew the guards' attention?

I looked at Jake and met his gaze. "I'm going to get you out of here. Then I need you to run like hell and hide." I thought about that. In theory Adak and Ghost should be tracking me. "You know who Adak is? The Dragon?"

His eyes went even wider and he paled, but the kid nodded. I had to give him props for that.

"Hide until Adak or a gray pit bull comes for you."

I could see the tremble in his lower lip when he spoke but he was doing his best to control it. "You're not coming with me?"

"If I can, I will but I might need to fight off the guards. You get out of here and wait for Adak. He'll get you back to your mom and dad."

The worms dropped to the ground. I didn't watch their transformation this time. I had to get this kid out of here. I could hear shouting somewhere on the floor above us. My time was up.

36

I DREW BACK and kicked out at the bar but the attempt was weak. Despite that, it sent pain through me that stole my breath. I couldn't kick my way through this one.

If I used my other foot, I wasn't sure I'd be able to walk at all. In fact, I had a feeling I wouldn't be able to balance on my bad foot to use the good one as a weapon.

I tried throwing my weight into my shoulder, but the bar didn't budge.

A lever. I needed a lever. I grabbed the piece of the bar I'd cut from my cell and wrenched it between the bars of his, then used it to apply pressure. Slowly, slowly, the bar began to give and bend.

The kid was skinny. If I could get the bar to bend enough, he could slip through.

It took precious minutes, but the bar gave, and the kid slid through.

But we were almost out of time. I looked around. There

wasn't much to work with. The hallway was mostly empty save for a pile of trash and old buckets in the corner nearest the door. I hobbled to it and lifted some of the debris.

Footsteps sounded on the stairs outside the dungeon. Heavy ones that indicated a lot of people running this way.

"Get under here. I'm going to draw the fight down the other way to distract them. You need to slip out the door and find your way out of here. Look for stairs and go up." My gut told me we were below ground.

Hiding Jake was a long shot at best, but it was all I had. I'd given the kid a chance, at least.

He nodded, shakily, and curled in a ball under the garbage and buckets. All around us, angry prisoners shouted for release. I backtracked down the hallway and did my best to balance on my bad foot, knowing I would need to at least put up a little fight if I was going to distract these guys.

Hopefully, they'd focus on me so they wouldn't realize the kid's bars were mangled before he had time to slip out. I gripped the bar I'd kept from my own cell and readied myself for a fight.

My heart sank as I watched thug after thug pour through the doorway and down the hall toward me. I can't imagine I looked very threatening standing with one heel up in the air, only the ball of my foot touching the floor.

I held the metal I was using as a staff in both hands and took on my best menacing pose. If it made them pause for just one more second before they attacked, it could be the difference in time Jake needed to escape.

The hallway worked to my advantage. They had no room to get behind me easily. With their fighting stances and weapons drawn, they only fit about three men wide.

If I wasn't careful, one could slip by me and take my back, but I wasn't about to let that happen. At least this way, I could take on no more than three at a time unless some of the guys in back had projectiles.

"So, y'all are going to be kindly gentlemen and attack one at a time to make this a fair fight, right?"

They didn't appreciate my humor.

I think they knew Gransen would be super pissed that I had escaped my cell on their watch and they weren't about to give me any leeway.

A guy with a mace came at me from the left, swinging his weapon in circles at the end of the chain. The guy in the middle had a sword and he closed the distance just as quickly as his buddy. I took a quick stab at mace guy's face, making him lean back to avoid losing an eye.

I used the back end of the makeshift bo and tried to catch sword guy between the legs. He blocked, stopping my attack at the same time a green bubble came floating at my face.

"What the..." I didn't get to finish my question before the bubble popped in my face, burning my eyes. It was like he threw acid on me.

And that's when I felt the tingling sensation. My bo was coming and it was coming fast.

37

Roxie

As my bo popped into my hand, I swung, unable to see, but not going down without a fight. My eyes ran with tears. I tried to hit where I remembered the thugs being before they blinded me. I connected a few times but had no idea what I hit.

My bo felt different this time. More solid, as if it had blended with the metal of the cell bar I'd been holding when it appeared.

If I wasn't under attack at just that moment, I might let the fascinating development distract me.

There were too many of them, even with my bo on my side. I heard the grunts as I found some of them and landed powerful blows. I heard the smack of at least one body hitting the concrete floor beneath us. But I couldn't take them all. There were too many of them and they'd done too much damage to me.

They overpowered me easily once I couldn't see. I took a hit to the side of the head, one to the ribs, and something sliced at my arm. I felt a continuous stream of pain and I cried out.

It felt like a million blows were coming at once. My body went limp, unable to fight back at all. As my body screamed in pain, I felt someone pull at my bo. I tightened my grip on the weapon, but it was useless.

The punishment came hard and fast, and when someone heavy stepped on my wrist, I couldn't stop my fist from opening. I felt them take my bo. It didn't matter. I knew from past fights, it would vanish the minute it was in someone else's hand and come back to me when I needed it.

This time, I didn't lose consciousness, but I only just stayed awake as two of them hauled me up and dragged me down the hall and up the stairs.

I tried to spot Jake as we went, but I didn't see him. Good. Hopefully he'd had enough time to make it out of the building and hide. Adak had to be here soon.

Confusion swamped me when I tried to figure out how much time had passed. Why wasn't Adak here yet? I'd told him the general area we were in, and he had Ghost to lead him right to me.

Gransen's men dumped me on the floor and I stared at the ceiling, sucking in air through lungs that screamed with each breath. My whole leg ached, not just my foot.

When I turned my head, I saw Gransen. I also saw what had to be most of his pack, encircling me. Three or four deep all the way around. We were in a large room. Not a bunker. Only a warehouse. I thought of the way Adak's people had torn the roof off of the last warehouse I'd been in.

Wouldn't that be a peachy scene to see right then?

Nah. Not waiting for rescue like a damsel in a story. I just needed a minute to get my strength and my breath back.

"You're the new partner at the plantation that was keeping

Mira and her kids as slaves?" I had no clue if I was right, but I was trying to stall.

Gransen didn't flinch or bat an eye at the word slave. It didn't bother him to be accused of treating people like property.

"I was going to expand our plantations threefold until that chimera got it into the nymph's head she could run."

I rolled to my feet, heavily favoring my good side, but standing tall just the same. "Why send the jinn? Why not go after her yourself?" I looked around. "You have a pretty big group here. Didn't think you could take the chimera?"

He lifted a lazy shoulder. "I wasn't ready for my involvement in that project to come out yet."

"So you gave Vivian the vessel so she could send the jinn to do your bidding but make it look like a zombie?"

Gransen gave a nod, but it wasn't to me. It was to one of his men. The guy smacked me across the face. Hard.

Ah, so he planned to play with his food before he ate it? Yay.

I looked at the goon who smacked me and then whipped my head forward, catching him in the cheekbone with it. I was satisfied with the crack I heard and the blood that now trickled from a split below his eye.

Gransen laughed. "My my, kitten wants to play."

I showed him my teeth. "Oh, we can play old man."

Gransen gave a flick of his hand and waved off the men who'd been holding me. "I'm going to make you pay for that insolent little mouth of yours. You're going to suffer for a long time. And then you're going to tell me what you know about the chimera and the nymphs. That chick and her brat are still valuable to me."

I realized he might not know I'd gotten Jake out of the cells downstairs yet. If his men had been focused on me, maybe none of them even knew the kid was on the run yet.

Good. That was good.

I hobbled to the right, making Gransen shift with me. It was subtle but just forcing him to make the move gave me a small mental advantage, especially in front of his people.

The flick of anger in his eyes showed me he'd caught it.

I widened my smile. "Let's get on with this, Gransen."

He was unbuttoning his shirt slowly, like he was going to put on some little show. As he did, he began to move in a circle. I fought the urge to circle with him the way I'd forced him to do moments before, and instead let him come around behind me.

It put him to my back, but I didn't care right now.

I listened for his attack, all the while scanning the area for anything that might help me in a fight.

A guy in the front row to my right had a bulky duffle bag at his feet. I might be able to grab the handles and use that as a projectile.

A woman on the left with crutches leaned heavily, resting her casted foot. I'd hate to knock a gimp down and steal her crutches, but I'd get over it pretty quickly.

Other than that, there wasn't a whole lot for me to grab. They had stripped me of my knives and stakes, but if I really got in trouble, my bo staff should come to me.

I heard Gransen move before he struck.

The side of his hand struck me in the neck, driving me down to the floor. It didn't hurt as much as it could have because I heard it coming and moved with it, but it still did damage.

I took an extra fraction of a second more than I needed to get up so he'd underestimate my abilities, but I didn't want to overdo it. Angela Bassett, I am not.

He kicked to my ribs, but I rolled and kicked out my foot to sweep his legs, managing to surprise him, but he knew how to fall.

We scrambled to our feet at the same time.

He threw out a jab and I weaved underneath, spinning and

landing a back-kick low in his gut. The move picked him up a few inches off the ground and bent his head forward. I took advantage with an elbow to his face.

But he recovered fast and glared at me. I'd been hoping he was all show with no real substance to him, but I was wrong. He might look like the Pillsbury doughboy, but he threw that weight behind each punch he threw.

Everything about him said he'd earned his position as the leader of one of Austin's largest and toughest packs the hard way. His position wasn't a trophy one.

Without taking his eyes from mine, he spat blood from his mouth and then grinned. That asshole grinned at me.

Before I could think too much about it, he was on me, apparently finished playing. He rained blows down on me so fast I didn't know what was coming from where.

His fists were sledgehammers. My head hit the concrete floor beneath us with a sickening crack that sent bile soaring to my throat. One eye was beginning to swell shut and I could taste blood in my mouth.

Fuck him.

Gransen winked at me, then looked to his people, arms raised, putting on a great display.

"Shall we play with water?" He boomed.

The crowd cheered and one of his people came out carrying sloshing buckets of water. She set the two buckets down in front of me and a sick light entered Gransen's eyes. He was going to enjoy this.

I was not. I didn't need him to tell me what was about to happen. Adak had already described Gransen's water trick to me. I knew he'd be using his water abilities to force that water into my nose and mouth, drowning me in a dry room.

Gransen walked my way, stopping in front of me and leaning down. When he spoke, it was low so no one around us could hear.

"You're probably asking yourself why this is happening to you." He affected a frantic voice. "Why me? Why would this man want to hurt me?"

I forced out a laugh at his mocking.

He came closer and spoke again, low. "I'm going to kill you slowly. I'm going to enjoy every minute of it."

He crouched in front of me now and I was getting my breath back. He'd been stupid to come so close to me. To underestimate me.

I reached out and fisted his shirt in my hands. Rolling to my back, I stuck my foot in his hip bone and tossed him over me, using his momentum to pull me up on top of him.

I crossed my arms and dug deeper into his collar, grabbing the back of his shirt to use it for leverage to apply a blood choke. Then I started to cut off the blood supply to his brain.

Blood chokes work fast. Unfortunately, I didn't have his arms restrained and unlike most people, Gransen didn't panic at this point. He grabbed my waist, throwing me off him with ease.

Gransen roared as he got to his feet and I saw the water rise from the buckets like two snakes, reaching for me. I tried to turn away, but it was fast and before I could stop it, the water powered down my nose and into my throat and lungs. I was choking on it, drowning, unable to breathe.

I tried to shove the water out, but it was no use. My body fought, desperate to suck in air only to find nothing but water.

And then it was leaving me, sucked out of me and back into the buckets as Gransen and his followers laughed.

I gulped for air, still choking on it even though the water was gone now.

My mind was screaming to give in, but I drew on the little bit of strength I had in me to climb to my knees and then my feet to face him again.

The water came again. I clawed at my neck, wishing I had

the strength not to give in and struggle like that, but I didn't. The panic that took over as my vision narrowed and black edged in was tangible and not something I was able to fight.

Gransen raised his hands again, playing to his crowd. "This is what happens when people cross me, isn't it? This is what comes from fucking with things you're told to stay out of," he called out.

The crowd cheered. He could have been reciting his grandma's recipe for oatmeal and they would have cheered. They were cheering the bloodbath, the violence. They obviously got off on it as much as their leader did.

The water came again. The sick prick was determined to make this last. He let me get a few seconds of precious air between each round. Enough to keep me conscious.

I vomited more than once. Not surprising.

His people were cheering, chanting his name, and taunting me. As the water rose again, my mind screamed out.

STOP!

And it did.

The water hovered before me, frozen in the air waiting. I would have said Gransen was holding it there, but I caught the momentary slip of surprise on his face before he hid it.

He pulled the water back, dropping it into the buckets before laughing off what had happened. I could see him scanning the room, trying to figure out who had dared interfere with his show. Questioning whether there was a witch in the room or if one of his own water dragons was strong enough to stop him.

I was trying to figure it out myself.

My bo staff appeared in my hand and I didn't hesitate. I took advantage of his confusion and struck. This time, my blows came faster than he could defend himself. This time, it was me pushing him back, forcing him to his knees.

And thank fuck, Adak and his people poured through the doors, Ghost barking somewhere.

The battle that ensued didn't last long. Before I could take him down, Gransen's people surrounded him, moving him to safety as they took his place.

The asshole ran, escaping in the protective bubble of his people who covered him until he made it to a truck.

Adak and his people fought at my back as I screamed out my rage at Gransen's escape. I'd had it with this man. I wanted him dead.

38

Roxie

"Are you sure about this?" Cristiano asked for probably the third or fourth time.

I turned to him. "It's the only way for you guys to keep hidden. People won't stop coming for them."

Adak and Ghost hadn't been able to track me to Gransen's underground prison because he'd paid for powerful wards on the building and land. But they'd been close enough that they found Jake and he was able to backtrack and show them where I was.

Cristiano and Mira had their son back, but as long as the magic burns were taking place, there would be a target on their backs.

When there was something that could make food suppliers money the way Mira and her boys could, there would always be someone gunning for them. And Cristiano couldn't hold out against them forever.

I was a realist. I knew this meant companies all across the

world were holding garden nymphs prisoner. I couldn't stop that. But I could help this family.

There was no point in me keeping the fold behind my cabin for myself because I thought I might use it someday. Not when he and his family needed it now if they were going to stay safe. The fold would mean no one could scent them or track them. It was their best chance for survival.

I looked down at Jake and Kallum who were scrubbing Ghost's side with their fingers, making Ghost run one back leg in the air like it tickled.

Jake grinned up at me. It felt good knowing I'd gotten him out of Gransen's clutches. I laughed to myself. Listen to me, I sound like an over-the-top narrator in some old movie. Gransen's clutches. I should go practice my mwah-ha-ha laugh in the mirror.

Wait, maybe it was the bad guy who does the laughing?

"We're more grateful than you can possibly know," Mira said, tears in her eyes.

I tilted my head up to see five dragons coming in for a landing. The fact they ferried a witch and a shifter on each shoulder told me they were Nova Force. That and I recognized Adak out front, the blue and teal of his scales glinting in the sun.

Adak had come ready for battle. I watched as a wolf and witch, who rode shotgun on his shoulders, slid down and they all shifted. The wolf was Tag and this time, Lesande stood by his side instead of her daughter.

I thought of a pirate when I looked at her. She had short spiky white-blonde hair and piercing brown eyes. She wore a scarf wrapped around her waist as a belt, the ends hanging down one of her jean clad legs.

There were five more dragons behind them, each of these hauling three or four witches. Sure enough, he'd brought the coven and then some with him in response to my request to stretch the fold and help with a plan to take out the jinn.

Lesande walked toward me. "Show us where the fold is. If the fires we saw on our way here are any indication, we don't have any time to waste in getting this family properly hidden."

I didn't tell her they'd been huddled in the small spot all day and we'd only decided to ask for help in stretching the fold after Adak and Nova Force had my back with Gransen earlier.

Several of her witches had been with Adak when he arrived at Gransen's prison earlier. They'd healed my wounds and healed the injuries of the other people we freed from the underground cells.

I showed Lesande to the fold and watched her slip through. She turned back and leaned out. "Send the others in."

Well, okay. I watched as more of the witches slid through. I wasn't sure how they'd all fit in there while they tried to stretch it, but I'd leave the details to them to work out. Maybe they had some clown car circus secret I didn't know about.

Three more witches stood on the outside but what caught my focus was Adak pacing several yards away from the house. He might be in his human form, but everything about him said coiled dragon ready to strike.

Tag left his side and headed toward me.

"What's wrong with the big guy?" I asked.

Tag didn't do anything to hide his amusement. "He's just having trouble adjusting to the fact not everything is under his control."

He meant me. I wasn't under his control. Poor dragon.

I couldn't help the grin that I directed at Tag. I don't know why it was so much fun to rankle Adak, but it was.

We turned to the witches who were chanting around Mira, holding a necklace out as they circled her. They'd scrawled runes on her arms and I could see a soft glow rotating through the runes, some lighting up before dimming as others lit up.

I didn't envy her. It was always nerve-wracking having

magic performed on you. Especially if you weren't a witch yourself.

It felt invasive and it could hurt like hell at times. I watched as wisps of green and yellow seemed to slip from her and into the necklace. And then they turned to me with it and I took a step back.

I'd come up with the plan. Asked them to do it. I was still jumpy though.

"I can have one of my people do it, Roxie," Adak said from behind me, making me jump and curse him all at once.

I didn't like it when people snuck up on me, least of all this guy, but I guess he had his mad under control again. Good for him.

I shook my head. "My vessel. My plan."

He put a hand to my back, holding me in place, with a grim nod. "They're just going to transfer some of her essence to you so the jinn will track you."

The witches began their chanting and one reached forward, slipping the necklace with its little blue and yellow beads over my head. The instant and steady ache that swept over me was no surprise. Magic sucked.

I winced and the witches all looked at one another before looking back at me.

"It shouldn't hurt," one of them said.

I raised a brow. "No?" What planet was this chick living on? All magic hurt. I stiffened and straightened up. "It's fine."

I could take it. I'd taken a lot more pain over the years. This was nothing.

The rest of the witches slipped out of the magic fold and Lesande and Adak seemed to scent the air.

"Good," Adak said with a nod. "Mira's scent leads here, and now you smell like her and read like her, magically. The jinn should come for you."

I watched as Cristiano said goodbye to Mira and the boys

before coming back to where we stood and shifting into his chimera form.

He raised his enormous head with a bone rattling roar, tossing his lion mane before letting it settle back over his shoulders, ready to protect his family.

That man was fierce. He really gave new meaning to King of Beasts.

"We need to get away from the fold so he doesn't stumble in there by mistake," Lesande said, shooing us all around toward the front of the cabin.

I pulled the stone vessel from my sheath and palmed it, ready to plow on with this insane plan. "All you guys need to do is let him get close enough to me to cut him with this and we'll have him."

We stood now in front of the porch, Adak's packmates fanned out around the front of the property, waiting for orders.

"The only trouble is," Lesande said, "we've made you smell like Mira and you have her magical trail, but he'll see you're not her the minute he gets here. He'll know it's a trap."

I looked down at the necklace. "Will he care? He'll figure I know where she is and that he needs to get to me to find her. Won't that be enough?"

"It's going to have to be," Adak growled, stepping closer to me as he pointed up the road that led to the cabin.

Flames. The jinn was here.

"Get Roxie close to him!" He called out as he plunged forward ready for battle. It was hard not to get distracted as he and the others shifted.

Their mythological forms were stunning, the witches all becoming taller and lithe. Shimmering magic hovered around them. Runes danced in light on their skin, telling the story of their magic as they readied for combat.

The dragons were magnificent— deadly and beautiful all at once. The wolf shifters leapt with such deft ease to the dragons' shoulders as they took to the air that it was hard not to stand and watch them all as they fell into formation in a dance they seemed to have done a thousand times together.

In the blink of an eye, a battle raged before me as the dragons swooped toward the jinn and the wolf shifters jumped at him, clamping down with jaws that would be burned and useless in a heartbeat if they didn't let go and run. They moved in fast, one after the other, so none had to hold on long.

Cristiano and I moved at the same time, shouting out a guttural war cry as we ran.

The jinn tossed aside the wolf shifters, who shook their dazed and damaged heads, whining as they tried to get back to their feet.

The witches hurled spells at the jinn and I realized they were trying to hit him with magical ice. It made sense. Hit him with the opposite of what he was.

We'd seen in the last battle that the fire and molten lava breathed by the fire and earth dragons did nothing to slow him down. Rather, it seemed to fuel him. To strengthen him.

Adak and the other dragons were hitting him from above, slashing with powerful claws and teeth that raked at him and seemed to slow him down.

Cristiano leapt and latched onto the jinn's middle with his powerful lion jaws.

I waited, watching for an opening to dive into the fray and use the vessel.

The jinn swatted at Cristiano, sending him flying. The witches had healed him, but maybe they hadn't given him all his energy back after the last big battle. I gave him credit though for jumping right back in after having his ass so thoroughly handed to him the last time. Then again, who was I to talk? I hadn't come out unscathed.

But right now I needed to focus on the fight ahead of us. I

just had to get close enough to cut the jinn. And not die doing it. That part was kind of crucial.

I didn't think I could sneak up behind him, even in all the fray. I was going down if the jinn stepped on me, or worse—sat on me.

How would that look on my tombstone? Here lies a dumb-ass, pancaked by a jinn.

Still, when in doubt, charge in. I ran forward, watching as the jinn slapped creatures off his body as if they were nothing more than mosquitos. Slight annoyances he could squash to stop the nibbling. The howls from the wolves as the jinn batted them rang in my ears but I shoved all that aside and kept moving.

The sky darkened, signaling the arrival of Gransen and his people. They wanted in on the battle. Or maybe he just wanted his jinn back.

I had the stone knife in my hand, blade pointing backward, pressed against my forearm. No sense in advertising my weapon.

Then I stopped. This was too obvious. I ran instead toward Lesande, palming the vessel and passing it off to her as I ran. I would distract him. She would make the cut.

I grabbed a knife from my sheaths and ran in a circle, drawing him away from Lesande.

The jinn's eyes fell on me, presumably finding me by my scent, because they widened in shock for just a moment before flaring in rage.

He realized I was carrying Mira's scent and knew we'd tricked him. I hoped it would cause him to make bad decisions.

No such luck. As I approached, he picked me up by the neck and slammed me onto the ground.

You don't really appreciate air until you can't get any into your lungs. And when a flame hand clutches your throat and your lungs feel like popped grapes, you really can't get any air.

He used one hand to pin me to the ground and the other to pin my knife hand.

He stared at me, eye to eye as if the rest of the world had disappeared. He didn't even notice the others, piling on like they could become a single force and take him out that way.

Lesande was moving in. She was five feet from his back.

Four.

I writhed in his grip.

Two. She had him.

He spun and grabbed Lesande up.

Now he had one hand on my neck and one on Lesande. He didn't go for her neck, though. He had his hand on top of hers where she held the vessel.

Nova Force struck at him from behind as Lesande screamed and used her free hand to hurl spells at him.

He was crushing the vessel, and her hand with it, then tossed her aside and turned back to me, his face inches from mine.

"You think to trap me with that broken vessel?" His voice was thick and monstrous.

He breathed into my face.

He twisted his head to the side, bringing the flames that were his mouth right up to lick at my cheek, searing my flesh. "Do you know what it's like, little girl, to have a jinn ride your body?"

I felt him shove his hips against me and clenched my teeth, fighting the pain.

"I'll slip inside you and burn you from the inside out. I'll walk around in your body for days, weeks, while you suffer and burn. While you watch me kill everyone you love."

The jinn seemed to grow until I was nothing to him. Until he was bigger than the dragons who still flew at him, trying to take him out.

I felt his flames kiss at my skin, then slip right under it. My flesh crawled and burned, bubbling under the onslaught.

I struggled, but he had me pinned. I had no way out of this. No way to save myself from the horror he was bent on carrying out.

39

ROXIE

THIS NASTY CREATURE would not take my body. I wouldn't give him the satisfaction.

It would be all too easy to let the disappointment wash over me. The vessel was broken and this vile creature was infesting my body. Nothing seemed to touch him. Nothing seemed capable of taking him down.

I wrenched my shoulders up, first one, then the other. I would not lie here and let him do this.

"Arhhhhhh!" The cry that came out of me was a battle cry. I would not give in.

One more inch. If I could turn, I could gain some leverage. I could fight back.

I *would* fight back.

The jinn released me with a guttural scream, his essence returning to his own body, but it wasn't my doing. I felt the void where he had been trying to enter me. My eyes quickly focused and took in the scene.

Adak!

He was in dragon form on the jinn's back, talons and teeth buried deep into the sides of the jinn's neck, and the jinn was having trouble reaching him to get him off.

Adak's whole body was lit with flame, but it wasn't the jinn's fire. It was Adak's. I don't know how I knew, but I did. And he was doing damage this time.

He was pulling fire from the jinn, making him shrink somehow.

Any moment now, the jinn would realize that all he had to do was stop, drop, and roll to remove the nuisance from his back. Guess he never saw those public service announcements Dash had watched as a kid.

I had to distract him.

I almost missed the tingling feeling that told me my bo was coming. But then I felt it. That telltale twitch.

"NOW? You show up NOW?" I shouted. "Where the hell were you thirty seconds ago when I was dying?"

I saw the broken vessel on the ground out of the corner of my eye. The blade was mostly intact even though the handle was dust at this point.

My shirt was already torn, so I finished the job, ripping off a strip from the bottom edge. I didn't know if the knife would still work in this broken state, but I had to try. I lashed the remaining part of the blade to the end of my bo as securely as I could.

I rose to my feet and began twirling the bo around me. Keeping it in motion would hopefully disguise the fact that I had attached the blade to it. If he thought the vessel was out of play, maybe he'd let his guard down and let me in close enough to put this to use.

I swirled it overhead, around my back, and to both sides, letting it float like magic through the air, creating a sort of shield around my body as I walked toward the jinn. I could hear its song as it moved and that music went straight into me, singing to me, steadying me. Getting me ready for what was about to come.

The jinn split his focus between me and Adak, which I hoped would give me the opportunity I needed to cut him. When he twisted around to reach for Adak again, I gripped my bo with both hands and slashed at the jinn.

The jinn moved too fast. I missed by a hair. I tried coming up from beneath him, but he dodged again.

He opened his mouth and let out a roar. Then he reached his arm back to prepare for a huge sweeping motion that would send me flying if it connected.

I launched my bo like a spear. It stuck into the jinn's chest and dangled there.

Dammit! I thought that would work. It had clearly cut him since the bo and what was left of the stone vessel were hanging from his chest.

What was I supposed to do now? Maybe there was a chant?

He reared his arm back again, clearly undaunted by the knife sticking out of him. I ducked close to the ground and covered my head to protect myself as best I could.

Nothing came. I peeked out to see the last wisp of orange and red flames disappearing into the stone.

I watched in stunned silence. I wanted to be sure he didn't come back out. Wouldn't that be a bitch if the part he'd broken off turned out to be the back door and he could just waltz back out to play?

Very slowly, I made my way over to where my bo had landed on the ground. I tentatively touched the knife blade, pulling it from the staff. It was warm and gave off a strong sensation of rage when I made contact. I slipped it into my pocket, unsure what to do with it and not ready to decide right now.

The carnage around me was devastating. Gransen and his dragons were on the run. He got a lot of practice at that.

I held my bo and watched as Adak's witches made the rounds, healing those they could.

Some were beyond healing. I counted three wolf shifters and a dragon who were dead. Witches couldn't raise the dead and even if they could, raising isn't the same as bringing them back to life.

Three witches bent over Cristiano. He was still. Too damned still.

I turned and ran to the fold, slipping through the magical entranceway. I stopped, too stunned to speak for a moment. The witches had stretched it so it could fit a small house if I wanted to have one built back here someday. But that wasn't what stopped me.

Mira and the boys stood in the center of the space waiting for news. She must have been trying to keep herself busy during the battle because the whole fold had been transformed into a natural wonderland.

Lush grass covered the ground and fully grown trees created a canopy up above. Where the sun broke through the trees, flowers bloomed in a virtual cascade of color and scent. I could smell jasmine and lilac, two of my favorite scents.

The far corner of the space held a small grove of fruit trees, already bearing fruit. Apples, lemons, pears, and cherries from what I could see. The small creek that ran through the back corner of my land ran through the fold, only it ran stronger here, creating a burbling backdrop to the oasis.

Mira twisted her hands. "Sorry, I create when I'm anxious."

Her words were enough to jar me out of my stupor. I waved an arm to call them forward with me. "The jinn is gone. Cristiano needs you."

If the witches couldn't heal him, she and the kids should be there with him.

Her face paled and she held her sons' hands tightly as they ran to me. We burst through the fold and back to the cabin, circling around it to where the battle had raged. Half of the woods were gone, but they'd managed to put out the fires. Adak was moving from person to person and the witches seemed to be down to healing minor nicks and cuts at this point.

I scanned the area where Cristiano had been.

There.

He was sitting up, looking over his arms at what looked like freshly healed burns.

Mira let out a cry and ran to him, the boys not far behind her.

The jinn was contained and Cristiano and his family were safe.

My grin faded when I looked to where the dead dragon and weres lay. I didn't know if they died in their human forms or animal forms but they were in their animal forms now. All myths transformed to their animal form upon death, as it was their true form. I didn't recognize them, but I didn't know most of the pack.

Still, they'd given their lives to have my back.

I closed my eyes. The pack had been involved because of me. I'd had blood on my hands for as long as I could remember. It had always been a part of who and what I was. I accepted that.

But I didn't have to like it, and right now, I really hated it.

40

ROXIE

THIS TIME when I went to Adeline's, it was by choice.

I looked up at Dagger Palace, as I'd dubbed the old brownstone building in my head. Dash was with his pack now so he was a lot less dependent on me, but I still needed money to support myself. Especially if I wanted to stay near him, which I did.

Didn't mean I was going to swear my undying love and loyalty to the vampire, but I'd see what she had to say.

The front door was open so I let myself in. The place was humming with energy as daggers moved from room to room, some looking fresh off a take down and others looking like they'd just come in for the day.

Dauphine came down the stairs toward me. "Ms. Andrews, a pleasure to see you. Congratulations on taking down the jinn. I assume you're ready to sign on with Adeline?"

Not really.

I smiled. "Something like that."

Dauphine's only response was a raised brow as she turned and gestured me up the stairs.

Everything looked much the same as it had before. Closed doors on the second floor, four zombies lining the top of the staircase leading to the third floor.

When we entered Adeline's parlor, there were only the two blond vamps tapping away on tablets. They glanced up and stood, leaving the room.

I had the eerie feeling everyone had known I was coming.

"Roxie," Adeline said like she was greeting an old friend.

I waited for her to say more but she didn't. Maybe there was some etiquette thing going on and I was supposed to be speaking now but I'd missed my cue.

The seconds ticked by but when Adeline moved, she did it at a normal pace, not the deadly mythical speed she was capable of. I guess whatever she expected of me, she didn't mind that I didn't offer it.

Color me shocked when Dauphine handed me a check.

"Payment for your work taking down the jinn."

I blinked and must have looked completely lost because Adeline explained.

"The city posted a reward for anyone who could stop the jinn. They announced it half an hour before you took him down, so I'm not surprised you didn't see it. They tried to backtrack when you got him into that vessel so quickly after it went up, but I took the liberty of having one of my people claim it on your behalf." She paused. "Less my cut, of course."

I smirked. Who was I to argue with her over that?

I looked down at the check. Sure she'd taken a big chunk of it, but I still got three thousand, four hundred dollars. Not bad for a payday, especially if I could count on getting more work through her if we could work out a deal.

I didn't need much to live on. Just a steady paycheck to buy food and maybe a little something to pay for cooking classes now that my brother's pack had destroyed my taste for canned Vienna sausages and dry cereal.

I folded the check and shoved it in my pocket. I wasn't about to eyeball that gift horse any longer than I had to.

"We need to talk terms."

She let my demand float out there a beat before a sly smile I didn't like graced her lips.

"Do we now?" The tips of her fangs were showing, a reminder of who she was and what she could do.

I held her eyes with mine. "If you want me to work for you, we do."

Dauphine glowered. Adeline laughed.

And then Adeline leaned in, her dead skin brushing my cheek as she whispered in my ear.

"Luckily for you, I'd like to have an Illieri warrior on my payroll."

ABOUT THE AUTHOR

In real life, Lori Collier is two people. Lori Ryan--a former lawyer and dog trainer who wishes she was a kick-butt dragon riding slayer of baddies, and Eli Collier--who actually is a kick-butt martial artist. She could probably be a dragon riding slayer of baddies if she could find a dragon who wasn't too grumpy to ride.

Lori Ryan lives with her husband, three kids, two dogs, and assorted other small creatures. She is a USA Today and NY Times bestselling author of romantic suspense and police procedural mysteries. She has over 26 novels and novellas out and has now begun writing contemporary romance, urban fantasy, and 1920s historical cozy mysteries with writing partners. She's absolutely convinced there's no better job in the world!

Eli Collier lives with her family in Nashville, TN. She holds a third degree black belt in MMA and a third degree black belt in Isshinryu. She was ranked 3rd in fighting and 4th in forms in the world for two years, and was inducted into the Universal Martial Arts Hall of Fame and the Isshinryu Hall of Fame as Competitor of the Year. When she isn't kicking things, she loves spending time with her dogs and feeding her sweet tooth.

www.ingramcontent.com/pod-product-compliance
Lightning Source LLC
Chambersburg PA
CBHW050024180626
46810CB00002B/568